DEVEL'S RENDEZVOUS
A Trilogy of Justice

A Chicago Story

By Reason of Birth

The Pride of Rhoidsville

by

Raymond Giovannelli

the PeppertreePress, LLC
Sarasota, Florida

Table of Contents

Preface

A Trilogy of Justice

Generally, three forms of justice exist:

1. **Judicial:** Arrest, formal charges findings of innocence or guilt, punishment that may include monetary reimbursement

2. **Street Justice:** Usually an act of hate, revenge, rage or injustice. Street Justice is considered to be very effective.

3. **Ecumenical Justice:** Perhaps the most accurate and powerful form of justice administered when the other forms of justice are false or failed. This also includes postbirth abortion and suicides committed to avoid responsibility for past crimes.

We must all answer to our maker.

Devel's Rendezvous

SECTION I

A Chicago Story

Chapter 1

April 12, 2001, 6:30 am
Chicago

A WOMAN STANDS AT HER FRONT-ROOM WINDOW WATCHING squad cars and unmarked police vehicles combing the neighborhood with their emergency lights activated. The woman, Nora Champi, has lived in the two-story building most of her life. The cops are investigating the bullet-riddled bodies of two of their colleagues. The scene is at a vacant lot at Halstead and Division streets in the neighborhood known as Cabrini Green.

It's dawn and while she quietly stands gazing into the early morning malaise of mist and emergency lights, her 50-year old wheelchair-bound son, Albert, enters the room. "Wow, you're up early, Al, and already dressed. I wonder what happened down there." Al is a Chicago Police Lieutenant, who suffered a stroke two years ago. Officially he is on disability leave, however, he continues to work with the Intelligence Unit investigating corruption within the department. The investigation of which Al has been an integral component is wide-ranging, targets include policy personnel, organized crime figures, and elected officials. It has been underway for a few years. Prior to his stroke, Al and his partner, Bart Ryan, were ordered to do a "black-bag job" on one Ron Stello, a low-level outfit bookie.

A black-bag job is an unauthorized, illegal wiretap. Al and Stello are products of Cabrini Green. During the 30s, 49s, and 50s, the neighborhood was predominantly Sicilian, but from the 60s to the mid-90s its population was primarily black. During both of these eras, it was one of the toughest, most violent areas of Chicago. In the early 2000s, the neighborhood has gone through large-scale gentrification. The Champi house is one of the few originals still standing.

Stello now lives in an apartment on the near Westside around Ogden and Grand avenues. Black bag jobs are not easy, whereas, court-ordered legal wiretaps are generally conducted directly from the phone company. In order to set up on Stello, Al and Bart had to get into his building, and locate the main telephone equipment box that services the place. Then they had to get into his apartment and with his phone off the hook, locate his line in the main box so a transmitter could be set on it.

While in the apartment they set up area transmitters throughout. All the transmitters operate remotely and transmit on an FM frequency. A car was then parked within a block of Stello's place, which contained a voice-activated tape recorder that was connected to an FM radio receiver, allowing for overheard recordings from the phone and the rest of the apartment. Tapes were changed and reviewed every four hours and the car was relocated a couple times a week. To make the surveillance complete, Al and Bart also planted a tracking and audio system on Stello's car. This would allow them to track the movement of the car and overhear conversation in and near it. This project went on for months, so that a voluminous amount of intelligence was gathered, including the locations of wire rooms and links between outfit members with public officials such as city aldermen and police personnel, specifically officers Jason Kucas and Danny Santi and Policy Department Personnel Manager, Christine Pesche.

Stello worked for the boss of the Westside faction, Tony "Tuna" Arcaro. Tony was Mafia, one of the few made guys in Chicago.

Chapter 2

While listening to a taped phone conversation between Ron Stello and Jason Kucas, Al and Bart overheard them talk about murder.

Stello stated that Arcaro wanted a young burglar, Steve Garzia, and his crew killed. Stello went on to explain that Garzia and company had burglarized Tuna's house. He wanted his goods back and, more importantly, he wanted Garzia and his guys punished.

Kucas indicated that he was interested, "I can do this thing, Ronnie." He set up a meeting with Stello for that night 10:00 pm at Halsted and Division to discuss the details. He told Stello that Danny Santi would also be there.

Al and Bart had a great view of the get-together, they had plenty of cover and there was a lot of heavy equipment in the area, because the city was demolishing the Ogden Avenue Bridge. The bug in Stello's car was working well.

A fourth person, Christine Pesche, showed up. Al recognized her immediately. Jason instructed her to sit and wait in her car. Stello questioned why she was there and Jason said, "She's our entertainment for tonight."

Al dated Christine when he started in the department. She was attractive then and remains so today. She was a little too flirtatious for Al's taste and he was especially turned off by her ménage a' trois with Jason and Danny in those days.

Al and Bart overhear Jason ask Stello, "What's this Garzia package worth to the Tuna?" Stello responds, "Twenty-long, but you gotta get all of his stuff back."

Jason responds, "OK, we're in for $20,000, now let's consummate the deal with some blow-jobs—hey, Christine get your ass over here." Al and Bart had ringside seats to the blowjob smorgasbord. Al mentioned to Bart that his dad used to keep a fishing boat in a makeshift slip on the river a few yards behind the location of the Kucas-Stello meeting place.

Follow-up investigation has revealed that Garzia and his crew burglarized a jewelry store that Arcaro had an interest in. The Tuna made Garzia return all of the loot to him, at his home. The episode pissed Garzia off to no end, so he and his crew burglarized the Tuna's home and took the loot back. Garzia had now crossed the line from "good burglar" to "dumb-shit." One by one the crew were killed, although Garzia's death involved some torture.

Al and Bart were ordered to stop the black-bag and get a court-ordered overhear. Their logs from the black-bag would henceforth be referred to as intelligence gathered from a confidential informant. If they were ordered to reveal the identity of their informant by the court, it would be the lately departed Steve Garzia. A task force was quickly formed consisting of the Chicago Police Intelligence and Internal Affairs units, and the FBI. The code name for this operation is "Devel's Rendezvous" (DRTF). Al picked the name, because his uncle owned a nightclub by that name on

Clybourn Avenue, about two doors north of Al's home.

On Friday nights, the Rendezvous was an impromptu meeting place for outfit wise guys such as The Tuna, and their flunkies, which included Jason Kucas, Ronnie Stello, and Danny Santi, and certain city aldermen. Several months after the hits on the Garzia burglary crew and obtaining the court-ordered overhear, Al and Bart listened to a conversation between Christine Pesche and Danny Santi. She told Danny that Internal Affairs and the Intelligence Unit were investigating the murders of some burglars. Danny asked, "Anybody we know working on this thing?"

Christine answered, "Do you remember Al Champi?"

"I sure do, but before we reach out for him, keep digging and report to me on a regular basis."

Al Champi was indelibly burned into the memories of Danny and Jason. Al had a younger brother, Carl, who was autistic and never advanced beyond the mentality of a seven-year-old. Nora tried to watch over him constantly, but on occasion Carl would slip away and walk through the neighborhood. Everybody knew the Champis and most of the time somebody would return him to Nora. Carl was obedient and harmless.

However, on one occasion he was collared by Jason and Danny. Jason was part of one of the few Greek families in the neighborhood and he was constantly trying to enhance his image with the neighborhood's premier street gang. Today he would attack Carl to impress some of the gangbangers. The exhibition began with Jason shouting ugly, insulting remarks towards Carl, who because of his autism was impervious to the attack. Jason now took their assault to the next level. He started slapping his victim around, and Carl began crying, covering his face with his hands, falling to his knees and begging Jason to stop.

That same day word of the incident got back to Al. Filled with rage, he left home via an old tunnel that ran under the sidewalk parallel to Clybourn Avenue, just in case any of Jason's gangbanger buddies were in the area. The tunnel was a long-forgotten remnant of Chicago's old sewer system. He emerged from the tunnel at Cleveland Street, about one block from home.

He found Jason and Danny on North Avenue. He walked up to Jason and without a word, landed a solid right hook to the jaw. As Jason went down, he tried to remove a 32-caliber automatic from his pocket. Al, reacting quickly, kicked the gun out of Jason's hand. Immediately he jumped on Jason, simultaneously grabbed the pistol, and started pounding him with it.

Jason, bloodied and hurting, blurted out through badly lacerated lips, "Shoot, asshole—ya don't have the balls do you? Come on, put one in my head, chicken-shit."

Al responded, "You want one in the head? You got it." With this, he ejected the ammo magazine from the pistol, popped one of the cartridges out, stuffed it into Jason's ear, and with his finger, shoved it as far as he could deep into the ear. Jason lay there screaming. Danny never spoke or moved. Jason and Danny certainly did remember Al—that beating became legend in the neighborhood.

Chapter 3

A FEW DAYS BEFORE THANKSGIVING, 2000, AL SUFFERED his stroke. As a result of the attack, he could not walk and had very limited use of his left leg, arm and hand. He was hospitalized for four months where he underwent physical and occupational therapy. Frequent visitors included task force members, Al's father, Carlo, who was divorced from Nora, and on a daily basis, Nora and Carl. Al's mom and brother remind him of a song, but he couldn't remember the title or the name of the lady who recorded it. He could only recall a few lyrics, "You and me against the world, it seems like you and me against the world."

Upon his release from the hospital, Al returned home wheelchair-bound. On his way home from the hospital, the van drove across the Michigan Avenue drawbridge. Whenever Al worked into the early morning hours, he would stop on the bridge, get out of his car, stand facing the East, and watch the sunrise. Before getting back into the car, he would wave to the bridge-tender.

Al and the other task force members decide to drop a leak regarding the Garzia murders, but this puts Jason and Danny in a tough fix. Tony Arcaro is pressuring them to find out what the hell is going on. They decide that it's time to go after Al, as they believe the stroke took a lot of fight out of him and they need to do something with heavy shock value.

It's Tuesday evening, Nora's grocery shopping day. Before heading to the store, she lets Carl stand outside in front of their home while she gets ready.

This same evening the Chicago Police department's 911 center received a call from a woman who claims a man tried to grab and fondle her while she walked past 1245 N. Clybourn Avenue. The caller described the alleged assailant as a white male, tall, and middle-aged. They also told the beat car to disregard. Jason and Danny reported that they were bringing the suspect into the precinct station.

When Nora went out to get Carl to go shopping, he wasn't there. She went on a hysterical search throughout the neighborhood, with no success.

Police records will indicate that the original complainant, a woman identifying herself as Linda Johnson, called at about 6:15 pm. Jason and Danny arrived on the scene at approximately 6:16 pm. At 7:45 pm an ambulance was dispatched to the precinct. Paramedics reported that they transported an unresponsive arrestee, Carl Campi, to Cook County Hospital. At 8:45 pm Carl was pronounced dead. The preliminary emergency room record indicated that the probable cause of death was blunt trauma to the head. Officers Kucas and Santi reported that Carl Champi became combative in the police station and had to be subdued.

Later an autopsy will reveal that Carl sustained serious injuries to the head, face, shoulders, upper and lower torso, forearms, fingers and legs. The head injuries were the cause of death; the injuries to the arms and fingers, which were fractures, were characteristic of defensive wounds.

Pursuant follow-up investigation, voice print comparison analysis, will identify Christine Pesche as the person who called 911. Later that night, Al's home was filled task force members. He was trying to console his mother. They were both on guilt trips—Nora because she allowed Carl to be outside unsupervised and Al because he was not around.

Nora asked Al to call his dad. Nora and Carlo have been divorced for over 15 years. He lives on the near north side with his second wife, Lika—she's a tough lady who had a terrible life prior to hooking up with Carlo. Several years ago Al rescued her from a bookie that she owed a lot of money to. Carlo works as a boat pilot for a boat touring company on the Chicago River.

Al opens the phone conversation with his father, "Dad, Carl is dead." Al waits for a response, none comes. He continues by giving Carlo all the details. Again Al waits for a response, he only hears what sounds like labored breathing and sobbing. All goes on, "The case is under investigation." Carlo finally speaks, taking a deep breath he asks, "How's Mom holding up?" "She's devastated, Dad." Carlo speaks again, "That kid couldn't hurt a fly!" "Let me know if you need me for anything."

The task force is busy fine-tuning its investigation in preparation for obtaining criminal complaints from the court or going before the Grand Jury for indictments. In either case, this first hurdle of getting the suspects formally charged is the easiest part of the prosecution process. The phases that follow, such as pretrial wrangling, strategic maneuvering, compromise, and finally trial, are much more tenuous and flimsy. Al's years in law enforcement taught him that going to trial is a 50/50 proposition. He thinks about those odds a lot when it comes to Jason and Danny.

It's been about two weeks since Carl's murder. Al receives a call at home—the anonymous male's voice is muffled and the background noise leads Al to believe the call is being made from a payphone. "Hey, wise up, cripple—remember dat movie when Richard Widmark tru dat old lady down da stairs in her wheelchair? Dat could be you." Al talked to his task force partners about the call and it's decided to initiate a stake-out on the Champi's home.

April 11ᵗʰ, 7:00 pm

While reviewing Tuesday's recordings of the current Kucas wiretap, Bart listens to the voice of a woman tell Jason that she is Al's mother. The caller states that Al is all she has left and will do anything to protect him. When Jason asked her how she obtained his phone number, she responded, "Off of the tape recordings and notes that the police have stored here. They do not want to leave this stuff at the P.D. If you promise to leave Al alone, I'll deliver everything to you." Jason asked her how soon she could get everything together. She said, "Right now."

Jason responds, "I don't like talking on this thing—meet me at midnight on the empty lot at Halsted and Division, and bring the stuff." The caller agrees.

Bart immediately alerts his surveillance team and instructs

them to tail Jason from home. He then contacts the team staking out Al's house to ascertain if they have seen anybody leave. They report that the only thing they have observed was Al being returned home by his physical therapist at about 7:15 pm.

Under the circumstances, Bart decided not to try and contact Al, because he doubted the authenticity of the call to Jason. First, the caller did not sound like Al's Mom. Secondly, the task force would never store evidence in any place other than the police department. To do so could very possibly break the very important chain of evidence. Bart now tells the surveillance team that's following Jason to give him plenty of room, because he'll be looking for a tail, so he tells them to stay loose. Another condition complicating the surveillance and good positioning is all the construction equipment parked in the area. There's a lot of work being done in the neighborhood and some of the streets are blocked because the Ogden Avenue Bridge was now demolished. The bridge used to span directly over the meet site.

One of the surveillance units reports that Kucas just picked up Santi and they are on the way. Surveillance teams watching the meeting site report seeing no activity and also that it's real dark. As Jason and Danny near the meet site, surveillance units pull back. The closest unit is a little more than a block away, and that unit has a view of the site, but not a good one.

Bart is situated about a block and a half away, but he doesn't have a good view either. Units now report the target vehicle has arrived. He has driven over the sidewalk and onto the empty lot on the corner and proceeds towards the back of the lot with his lights out … "We see brake lights, so he must have stopped."

Bart instructs the surveillance units to sit tight and wait for the other players in this meet to show. Traffic is at a light volume and it's a few minutes after midnight. The closest surveillance unit reports, "I see flashes—they look like muzzle flashes and I hear popping that could be shots, lots of them."

Bart also hears it and realizes that the sound is obviously fully automatic weapons, so he commands, "Move in, everybody … move, move, move! I want the team on the Champi place over here, too—NOW!"

Surveillance units are on the site in less than a minute, while DRTF officers cautiously proceed on foot. Bart's team finds Jason's car, both front doors are open and there's a body on the ground with his legs still in the car on the passenger side. With the help of flashlights, one can see that each body has been shot many times.

Bart orders the task force members to sweep the immediate area for suspects and get some patrol units out to do a wide sweep. His group cordons off the area for evidence technicians. With his flashlight, Bart finds numerous 9 mm expended cartridges. Ejected cartridges in numbers like this are indicative of fully automatic weapons. This was a perfectly executed ambush.

Bart can't wait to tell Al that Jason and Danny have been wasted, but he's just too busy right now. For an instant, a bit of irony crosses Bart's mind—the fact that the scene is the location where this case practically began, Halsted and Division streets.

After two hours of searching, task force members are starting to think that maybe they are looking for ghosts, demons, or the Devil himself, because the surveillance teams entered the site from every direction within 30 to 40 seconds, except from the southeast, but there's nothing there but river.

Another puzzle challenging investigators is that surveillance teams were in position at the scene within half an hour after the call was heard. Nobody was observed entering or leaving the area until the arrival of Kucas and Santi. Patrol units checked the river from both directions for about two miles as best as they could from the street, but they observed nothing. Later, voice print comparison analysis will reveal that Nora was not the caller—the analysts will say they believe the caller may have been a woman probably disguising her voice, but they are not sure.

At about 5:00 am, the Michigan Avenue Draw Bridge operator arrived at his control tower to start his shift. The tower operates daily between 5:30 am and 10:00 pm and right now, dawn is breaking. As he uncaps his paper coffee cup and turns his portable radio on, he notices a man running up the bridge stairs from the riverside below. The fellow looked familiar. Just as he reached street-level, a dark-colored flat-bottom fishing boat, about a 12-footer, emerges from under the bridge heading east on the river towards Lake Michigan. The guy on the bridge waved to the driver of the boat, who looked like an old man, big with white hair. The man on the bridge stayed for a while and watched the boat leave. Leaning, with both hands on the bridge rail, he stared eastward looking at the early sunrise.

Rush hour traffic had not yet begun, as the man on the bridge hailed a cab. When it stopped, he ran over to it. Before getting in, he looked up at the bridge tender. The cab drove off northbound on Michigan Avenue. As the bridge tender watched the cab drive away with its tail lights glowing, a song by Helen Reddy started playing on his radio. The song was You and Me Against the World: "And when one of us is gone and one of us is left to carry on, then remembering will have to do, our memories alone will get us through."

Justice in this case is commonly referred to as
"STREET JUSTICE."
It's not legal, however, it's very, very effective.

SECTION II

By Reason of Birth

Introduction

Scientific evidence has been mounting, which indicates that most of the universe is "Dark Matter" or "Dark Energy." This energy is intrinsic in the cosmos, that being galaxies, stars, planets, human beings, dark areas, and all living organisms. In terms of human existence, Dark Energy is in a constant cycle of introgression from pure energy to people; then back to pure energy pursuant to death, at which time it is extricated from the dead human body with the assistance of close ancestral Dark Energy.

In its dark form it consists of numerous generations of hereditary groupings bearing their own genetic codes and lineage.

The human species is perpetuated in large part by the transmission of Dark Energy during the time of conception. In very rare instances, it occurs during a "Near Death Experience" or NDE.

Many NDE patients claim seeing a bright light and hearing voices during unconsciousness. What they are experiencing is the presence of the most opportunistic Dark Matter. This event connotes an aggressive transference of Dark Energy that is on a mission.

Chapter 1

Paramedics are responding to a 911 call in the affluent Chicago suburb of Kenilworth. The call came from the home of Frank Corsini, the wealthy CEO of Windy City Realtors. Frank is widely known for his reputation as one of the most successful commercial real estate brokers and developers in the Chicago area. His wife, Sarah, and business associate, Barry Katz, are present when the paramedics arrive.

Frank is laying on the floor of his study; he is unconscious. His heart rate and blood pressure are dangerously low.

Chapter 2

FRANK IS 55 YEARS OLD AND HAS ALWAYS BEEN A STICKLER for physical conditioning. He works out at least five times a week in his fully equipped, at-home health spa. A large portion of the eleven thousand square foot home includes everything from the latest state-of-art conditioning machines to a sauna, steam room, and whirlpool.

Frank has been married to Sarah for fifteen years. She is 20 years younger. Their fifteen–year-old son, Nick, is attending school in Italy.

Frank was the only child born to Nella and Nicholas Corsini, second-generation Americans. Ancestors of both Nella and Nicholas came to America from Florence, Italy. He was raised in a well-to-do north-shore suburb of Chicago. He led a privileged life, and was overprotected by his family. He was introduced into the business at a young age. Frank graduated cum laude at twenty years old, with a double major in business and architecture, from the Prestigious Northwestern University in Chicago. He never had the opportunity to play or develop street sense.

Sarah's maiden name was Levi. She was raised in a middle-class Chicago suburb. Sarah and Barry were neighbors. They lived in the Six Flat apartment building, owned by Sarah's

Uncle Irving Goodman. Barry's dad, Sal Katz, was a sales representative for Windy City Reality. Sarah and Barry were given jobs at the company after they graduated high school.

Barry worked with his dad as a sales apprentice, while Sarah worked as a clerk typist in the downtown office. It was about this time that Nick Corsini decided to retire and turn the business over to his son. While Frank was developing his business style and acquiring a positive reputation as an honest businessman, Barry grew into a successful sales representative.

Frank met Sarah when she was nineteen years old. She worked at the company's downtown Chicago office. Frank didn't spend a lot of time in the office—he was out in the field at construction sites. He usually didn't get into the office until late in the day, and really didn't see or think about the attractive clerk typist, who was sexy and flirtatious toward men. But Sarah thought a lot about Frank. She thought about him even when she was being intimate with Barry. She tried coaxing Barry into introducing her to Frank, but Barry couldn't picture them as an item.

Sarah and Barry talked about the company frequently. Barry was critical of Frank's business style. He thought Frank was too soft for a CEO. On several occasions he took it upon himself and rescinded Frank's decisions.

Sarah took matters into her own hands and came on to Frank at the company's Christmas party. Sarah flirted with Frank. She was extremely attractive; curly black hair, green eyes, and shapely. She was not a tease—she was promiscuous. She enjoyed pleasing men, and whether he was Jew or Gentile, he was in store for a good time. She played Frank like a violin, teased him, and when she was sure she had his attention, she suggested that they move into the privacy of his office. She had him where she wanted him. He was aroused. She was ready.

In his mind's eye, he pictured this young, attractive woman on his desk. They were both drinking, everyone was having a great time. What was happening? She was nineteen years old and he was forty. Although it was difficult, he dismissed her advances, got back to reality, and rejoined the party. He had to cool down and always be mindful about who he was.

Coffee and cake were served to sober the revelers up. As the festivities were winding down, Sarah approached Frank and apologized for her behavior, explaining that she had too much to drink. Could he forgive her and drive her home? Frank agreed.

She asked Frank to park in a nearby school lot for a few moments before he dropped her off, it was about 11:00 pm. When they parked, she moved close to him and started gently kissing his neck, face, and ear. She began fondling him, unzipped his pants, reach inside and fondled his shaft. Was this the same Sarah who worked as a clerk typist in his downtown office? Now he was completely aroused and slipped his hand under Sarah's dress. He slowly moved his hand between her legs and discovered she wasn't wearing panties. She was soft, warm, and very wet—his erect penis was now protruding outside his trousers.

She gave him oral sex and started asking, "How do you like it, Frank, slow, fast? Tell me what you want—do you wanna fuck?" Frank didn't have time to answer, as she raised her dress above the waist, lifted her right leg over, so she could straddle him, with her right hand, she guided his penis into her and slid up and down on his very hard shaft. He remembered the package of condoms he carried in his wallet. He tried to push her off to get to his wallet. She told him "Don't worry about it," so he assumed she was on some form of birth control. He could not hold off any longer, so he told Sarah he was ready to cum. She put both hands on the roof of the car and pushed herself down on him for maximum penetration, while at the same time frantically rotated around Frank's exploding penis.

A few weeks later, she told Frank that she was pregnant with his child. He did the honorable thing and they were married.

Chapter 3

EMERGENCY ROOM DOCTORS ARE FRANTICALLY TRYING TO raise Frank's blood pressure and heart rate; doctors feared that if his vital signs did not normalize soon, he would die. By all outward appearances he seemed to be unconscious, however, he could hear and sense the presence of the people in the ER.

The only thing he could see was an extremely bright light. At first there was just darkness. Then a faint light appeared. It was as though he was in a long tunnel and a speck of light was at the entrance. The speck of light came closer and closer—then it became brighter until it was all-consuming. His inner vision was engulfed by its brightness. Suddenly Frank heard a voice, "Doctor, pressure and heart rates are normalizing." Someone lifted his eyelid and the bright mysterious light that had been dominating his inner self disappears instantly and is replaced by a doctor's examination light.

Frank hears another voice, "Starting to look a little better, but he's still in danger." Then a woman's voice, "Oh please, God." He recognized the voice immediately as Sarah.

What seemed like an hour or so in the hospital has in reality been over 24 hours. First in ER and eventually in ICU, Frank is still displaying the characteristics of unconsciousness and his doctors are concerned. Tests and examinations have led to a preliminary diagnosis of Acute Ischemic Stroke.

In a rare moment, Frank senses that he is alone in his room with Sarah, so he decides to open his eyes and surprise her. But at that instant, he hears her dialing the phone. Sarah asks to speak to Barry Katz. Frank assumes she is going to give Barry an update on his condition.

In a low, but understandable tone he hears, "Hi, Baby, he's about the same, but I miss you, too. Oh stop it, here I am sitting on deathwatch and all you can think about is BJs." She hangs up, but Frank's heart is now pounding—all he could hear were his own internal screams. He experiences a new sensation—RAGE.

A few minutes after Sarah left Frank's room, his neurologist walked in to conduct a status check. As the doctor approached, Frank moaned and opened his eyes. The doctor smiling broadly said, "Well, Rip Van Winkle has finally awakened."

For the next four or five hours Frank was examined by several doctors who were assisted by technicians. His ICU room was a flurry of activity. The neurologist informed Frank that he had suffered a stroke. A clot caused blockage to the right side of his brain, consequently, he should expect some paralysis to the left side of his body. Frank realizes he has lost power and mobility on his left side.

Throughout the days, weeks, and months that followed, which were filled with exhaustive, painful tests and procedures, he started to notice shifts in his pattern of emotions, for example, from timidity and passiveness to impatience and aggressiveness. He also changed from anxiety and concern for what others may think of him to fearlessness, suspicion, and disregard for the feelings of others. What concerned him most was this new emotion that uncontrollably surfaced when Sarah and/or Barry visited—RAGE!

Frank had time to think. He thought about what a fool he had been—he was so naïve. Prior to the stroke he would have blamed himself for Sarah's restlessness—he would have believed it had to have been his fault. What mistakes did he make? Now something from deep within was telling him something different. He looked back on his life with Sarah. He was *not* the problem. How could he have been so blind to their connection? What are they planning? What he is feeling is uncontrollable, it has a life of its own—is he suffering some form of psychoneurosis?

Chapter 4

Frank is assigned to a room on the rehabilitation floor where he undergoes various physical, occupational, speech/cognition, and psychological tests and treatments. The assessment tests reveal that Frank would not require speech therapy. Cognitively he was rated 100%. His therapist would remark that "He is as sharp as a tack." He would spend 40% of his time in physical therapy, 20% time in occupational therapy, and the rest of his time would be spent in psychotherapy.

Dr. Amber Wallace, the unit psychologist noted that many stroke victims undergo certain personality modifications, usually as a result of depression. However, in most cases these psychological anomalies are detected and brought to light by family members and/or friends. In Frank's case, he expressed great concern over deeply rooted emotional impulses that "seize his soul."

Windy City Realtors deals primarily in commercial properties. It is a wholly-owned corporation, with the Corsinis owning all the stock. The business was initially organized into three divisions: building and development; sales and rentals; and property management. When Frank became CEO, he reorganized the business into two divisions:

commercial real estate sales and rental management. The newly restructured company hit the ground running. Windy City Realtors became one on the largest commercial property developers in the Great Lakes area. A few years after Frank took over the company, he promoted Barry to president of the commercial real estate sales division. Frank could now focus on the rental management division. He could concentrate on growth opportunities in property acquisitions and new construction. In order to accomplish his goals he promoted Sam Goodman, engineer/architect, to vice president.

Chapter 5

DURING THE FIFTEEN YEARS ENSUING THE MARRIAGE OF Frank and Sarah, and the restructuring of Windy City, a symbiotic relationship arose between Sarah, Barry, and Sam. This union was mutually beneficial for the three, but not for the unsuspecting CEO-husband. Barry and Sam, using Sarah as a direct pipeline to Frank, helped advance some of their personal plans and business ideas. As for Sarah, she was more than willing to be used, since it allowed her to get involved at the very top of the business.

The other factor in this alliance was the steamy intimacy between Barry and Sarah. They were careful to keep the affair discrete; however, Sam was aware of it. The three grew up together and were friends long before their involvement in Windy City. Sam's father was the owner of the Six Flat where they all lived. Additionally, Barry would frequently regale Sam about Sarah's sexually promiscuous talents. Whatever respect or gratitude Sam and Barry had for their boss diminished over this period. The business systems and ethics between them and Frank were diametrically opposed.

Expediency and arrogance fueled the business methods of Frank's two top executives. He argued with them frequently about arbitrary firings, evictions, and other improprieties such as careless bribing public officials and withholding payment to subcontractors for opportunistic reasons. Sam and Barry considered Frank a myopic fool, not only in his business, but also his marriage. He was clueless about Sarah's affair with Barry. She would frequently convince Frank that he should rethink his position when Sam or Barry presented a new ideas.

Chapter 6

FRANK REMAINED ON THE REHABILITATION FLOOR FOR several weeks, his physical and occupational therapists reported excellent progress. However, Dr. Wallace informed the rehabilitation physician and other therapists that she had decided to refer him to a psychiatrist. She believed that Frank was suffering from a form of psycho-neurosis and she did not have the experience or skills necessary to psychoanalyze him. Frank feared that he could not control the compulsions or obsessions that raced through his mind. He came to grips with the possibility that he was ill and he needed help.

Dr. Wallace referred Frank to Dr. Ian Stenson, formerly the head of Psychiatry at the University of Illinois and currently the Director of Personality Studies at Northwestern University in Illinois. Dr. Stenson agreed to take the case. He is a world-renowned psychiatrist, however, over the past several years he has devoted his time and expertise to research rather than psychoanalysis. Dr. Amber knew there was a good possibility that he would accept the case, because the focus of his current research is near death experience.

Chapter 7

Frank was released from the hospital approximately four months after his stroke; he was sent home wheelchair-bound. Sarah made arrangements for him to begin physical therapy at a rehabilitation center near his home. Dr. Stenson scheduled his psychoanalysis. Sarah hired a male nurse to help care for him.

Within two weeks of Frank's homecoming, Sarah arranged a party at the house. Her guest list included business associates and public officials. At this lavish black-tie affair, Frank, although wheelchair-bound, circulated around the party. He was pleased with his ability to suppress his anger and hate, especially when he was around Barry, Sam, and Sarah. He surprised himself with the ease in which he masked those emotions with cordiality and the appearance of gaiety.

Sarah controlled the guest list, however, there was a young woman at the party whom she didn't recognize. She asked Frank discretely, "Frank, do you know that pretty lady?" He told Sarah that he would introduce her later. At dinner when everyone was seated and all the toasts were made, Frank introduced Wendy Olson, his personal physical therapist and assistant. He leaned over and whispered to Sarah that he fired the male nurse and cancelled therapy at the Rehabilitation

Center. With a smile on his face he gently took Sarah's hand in his and continuing to whisper, telling her that he would get his physical therapy at home with Wendy. The therapist was an extremely attractive woman in her late 20s. Frank had met her at the Rehabilitation Center. She was a part-time physical therapist there. After whispering his message to Sarah, he gave her a gentle kiss on the forehead. A few days after the party, Frank moved into a separate bedroom. He would get his physical therapy in his work out area. Wendy's living arrangements were in a bedroom nearby.

Chapter 8

ON THE DAY OF FRANK'S FIRST SESSION WITH DR. STENSON, Sarah walked into his bedroom. Frank was being towel dried by Wendy. Sara offered to drop him off at the doctor's office on the way to her bridge club meeting. He told Sarah not to worry about it, Wendy would drive him.

It the first meeting, Dr. Stenson asked Frank to discuss his family. The doctor wanted to know as much as Frank could tell him about his ancestry and lineage. Frank explained that he was third-generation American and had no siblings. To the best of his knowledge his ancestors migrated from Florence, Italy. His mother's maiden name was Soderini, but he did not know the maiden names of his grandmothers. He did not believe there was any history of mental illness in his family.

Dr. Stenson then asked to describe the sensations he experienced on the day of his stroke. Frank explained that there was no pain. What he remembered the most was the gradual emergence of a very bright light. He talked about the fact that he could hear everything that was going on in the emergency room. He informed the doctor that he believed that he could have opened his eyes at any time, but something inexplicable compelled him to feign unconsciousness. Frank then told the doctor about Sarah's telephone call to Barry from his ICU room.

Frank's mention of the phone call and the insidious rage that followed, segued into the doctor's last question for this session, "Frank, why do you believe your personality is changing? Think about that and we will talk about it next time."

Dr. Stenson's most recent work focuses on what Frank had just gone through, his "Near Death Experience." Most of the people the doctor has interviewed talked about a bright light. Many of them claim to have talked to voices within the light. The voices said they were waiting to be reincarnated.

Dr. Stenson's research into NDE has also led him into the study of reincarnation. He believes that reincarnation is a natural cyclical process that occurs in two ways. The prevalent occurrence involves the transference of energy from a previous life into the embryo during conception.

The second is exceptionally rare; it involved the transference of previous life energy during a NDE. This intervention and simultaneous occupation of a body is carried out by energy best characterized as aggressive and daring. It can have considerable influence on the personality of the individual it has chosen. Dr. Stenson believes that all reincarnations are regulated and directed by ancestry, i.e., lineage that can span many centuries. However, the doctor will treat Frank with conventional psychiatric methods. He will not corrupt the psychoanalysis of his patient with his research of near death experience.

Chapter 9

WENDY GIVES FRANK PHYSICAL THERAPY EVERY MORNING. The only medication he is on is Coumadin, a powerful blood thinner. He gets his blood checked every six weeks to make sure that the anti-coagulant levels in his system are appropriate. Taking too much of the medication could be disastrous

Every day Frank and Wendy go to his downtown office, where he meets with Barry and Sam regularly. It is getting more and more difficult to mask his disgust for them. Sam informed Frank about a new commercial development, a large strip-shopping plaza located in an old neighborhood. Sam indicated that he and Barry are working out the details. Frank asks, "Sam, how's your rapport with the city inspectors in that district?" Sam's response is a smile, a wink, and the thumbs up gesture.

Before leaving Frank's office, Sam asked for a sizeable advance of $150,000. He tells Frank that he has been living beyond his means and needs to get back on track without making his wife and kids suffer. Frank issued a personal check, but instructed Sam not to deposit it for at least a week. When Frank is alone, he telephones a friend at the Attorney General's office. He advised his friend that he would like to set up a meeting to discuss pay-offs and bribes to city inspectors.

Chapter 10

FRANK IS IN DR. STENSON'S OFFICE—THIS IS THE MEETING he was not looking forward to. Dr. Stenson asks Frank, "Would you be more comfortable on the armchair or sofa, or would you rather stay in your wheelchair?" He tells the doctor that the wheelchair is fine. "Well, Frank, have you given any thought to my question about whether or not you feel that our personality has changed?

Frank nods yes. He reasons to the doctor that the personality shifts are probably due to a combination of events: first the depression, realizing that the left side of his body may be dead as a result of the stroke, so maybe it's a form of mourning. Secondly, the discovery that his wife has been unfaithful is certainly a part of the change.

Dr. Stenson agrees that the experiences Frank talked about were powerful enough to alter his personality. However, he needs to have Frank tell him about his personality profile before the stroke, beginning with his childhood.

Frank was an only child and was pampered by his parents and grandparents. He was raised in an upscale economic environment. He never wanted for anything. He attended parochial elementary and high schools. He graduated from college with double majors—he was always an above average student in terms of grade point average.

As far as business is concerned, he considers himself a no-nonsense, but benevolent CEO. He informed Dr. Stenson that his two top executives and wife constantly criticize him for not evicting tenants who, for whatever reasons, are delinquent with their rent payments.

The doctor asked, "Why don't you evict them?" Frank's response is that his tenants all pay rents that are higher, in comparison to other commercial locations. When he negotiates lease agreements, he never waivers on his price, therefore, his tenants are paying top dollar. In Frank's opinion, a businessman can survive with a reputation of being stubborn and stingy, but he cannot risk being hated by evicting tenants or confiscating their property. Exhibiting honesty and humanness in his business is a formula for success. Frank's comments regarding his business manner struck a familiar chord with the doctor. Where had he heard this before?

Frank tells the doctor, "What bothers me the most is the RAGE I feel when I'm in the company of Sarah, Barry and Sam." He told the doctor that it's probably a good thing that he is confined to a wheelchair because if I was 100% physically, I might do something foolish."

The doctor asked, "When you say foolish, what do you mean, Frank?"

Immediately becoming illusive, he responds, "Hell, I don't know what I meant, doctor." The doctor informed Frank that they would discuss anger and rage at the next session.

For the rest of the day Dr. Stenson tried to recall where he had heard or what he may have read that reminded him of Frank's remarks about his business style. One of the doctor's minors in school was business—perhaps that was the key?

Chapter 11

FRANK SUMMONED WENDY FROM THE DOCTOR'S WAITING room. Wendy seemed stressed this morning. After transferring him from the wheelchair to the car, he instructed her to take him to the Attorney General's office in the State of Illinois building.

Before she started the car, Frank looked at her and told her that she looked downhearted. "Is everything OK?" he asked. They were together every day, all day, and the look of despondency was uncharacteristic for this young, pretty lady.

She started to tell Frank that even though she has only known him a short time, she felt very connected to him, but Frank interrupted her, "What's up Wendy?"

Wendy said very quietly, "I think Sarah and Barry have something going on."

Frank asked, "What makes you think that?"

She explained that he's always in the house with her, and on one occasion she observed them in the indoor pool area and it looked like they were fondling each other.

Frank couldn't help cracking a peevish smile. Suddenly he felt himself make a facial expression he has never done before. He arched one eyebrow and while looking at Wendy with a sneering smile, he told her that he trusted them. However, he shocked himself with what he blurted out next, "But if they are fooling around, maybe you can console me with a grudge fuck?"

Wendy smiled, started the car, and said, "Maybe."

Chapter 12

THE ATTORNEY GENERAL, WILLIAM REED, IS A TWO-TERM Republican. The Corsini family has supported him with generous political contributions, so Frank gets a personal meeting with the boss. After exchanging greetings and small talk about Frank's stroke and wheelchair existence, Reed asks, "What's up?"

Frank explains that he thinks that one of his top-ranking executives is routinely bribing City Building Inspectors and in doing so, runs the risk of destroying the reputation of the Corsini family.

The Attorney General sits quietly for several seconds and then asks, "How can I help?"

Frank proposes that the Attorney General's office set up a sting. "Bill, he said, if you will do this, I'll take care of the rest of the situation."

The Attorney General made it clear to Frank that what was being proposed was out of the ordinary, because cases such as this are usually initiated with criminal prosecution in mind—not the convenience of private enterprise. Bill rose from his desk chair, walked around his desk, shook Frank's hand and said, "However, consider it done, my friend." He told Frank that investigators would contact him to fine tune the operation.

Frank and Wendy returned home to find Sarah and Barry enjoying cocktails. They were not inebriated, but it was obvious that they had been hitting the bottles for more than the normal cocktail hour. Sara liked dry gin martinis, while Barry's choice was scotch on the rocks.

Frank always thought it interesting that Barry drank so much because he suffered from ulcers. Although he consulted with a particular specialist over the years, he went out of his way to avoid scheduled treatment. Barry told Frank that when you become dependent on doctors, "You're a dead man."

The manner in which Barry and Sarah talked to each other, combined with glances and body English, would suggest to even unsuspecting observers that they were more than cocktail-swilling friends.

Frank concluded that he must do whatever it takes to prevent their affair from becoming widely known. He thought to himself, "The Corsini name and reputation must be protected at all costs." He insisted on mixing a couple of rounds that evening, because he was setting the stage for future, daily cocktail hour get-togethers.

Chapter 13

THE NEXT DAY AFTER WENDY DROPPED FRANK AT THE office, he instructed her to pick up his Coumadin refill. He then told his secretary that he did not want to be disturbed by anybody. From an elaborately concealed bar in his office; Frank obtained a bottle of Scotch, put some ice in a glass, and poured a double shot. He then added three finely crushed Coumadin pills, five milligrams each, to the drink; the Coumadin material dissolved quickly and completely. Frank's therapeutic dosage of the powerful blood thinner was one, five-milligram pill per day. Great care had to be exercised when using this medication.

After completing the Coumadin cocktail-making experiment, he told the secretary that he would accept calls and guests now. Prior to lunch, Frank received a call from an investigator with the Attorney General's office informing him that a meeting was scheduled within the hour at the State of Illinois building. There were four AG agents at the meeting. Frank filled them in on the location of the new job site, Sam's full name and description, his home address, and car description. They were going to try and make the sting as soon as possible.

When Frank returned to the office, he called his bank

and put a stop-payment order on the $150,000 check he had given Sam. He then called Dr. Stenson's office and cancelled his next appointment, indicating he would call at a later date to reschedule.

That evening Frank summoned everyone down to the grand room for cocktails. He had already mixed the first batch and watched with satisfaction as Barry slurped away and smacked his lips in approval. In the days that follow, Barry will ingest about fifteen milligrams of Coumadin per day.

Chapter 14

Two days after the meeting between Frank and the Attorney General's investigators, Sam was arrested and taken to a holding center. During an informal critique Frank was told that the sting went down like clockwork. Arrangements were made for him to sit with Sam in an interview room.

During the interview, Frank told Sam he would do everything in his power to protect him and his family from the embarrassment of criminal charges, trial, and publicity. Frank then stated he was forced to terminate Sam's employment and had placed a stop payment on the $150,000 advance.

Sam slumped down into his chair and began weeping, "Frank, what am I going to do? Creditors are ready to knock my door down. I'll lose everything, my home, my wife, my kids—oh, God, Frank, please, please!"

"Sam, aside from not pursing criminal charges, there's nothing more that I can do."

Sam's wife, Leda, is the daughter of two doctors. Her father Ira Slayman, is a gastroenterologist. He is the doctor who has been treating Barry Katz for his ulcers. Her mother is an obstetrician. They both have extremely successful practices. Leda is high maintenance, an incorrigible socialite and spending machine. All their married life, Sam has been over his head in debt, trying to satisfy her lifestyle. Frank has taken into account all these circumstances, which will soon prove beneficial.

Chapter 15

FRANK REALIZES THAT A PART OF HIM ENJOYS BEING deceitful to accomplish his purpose. He is languishing in the efficient ruthlessness now guiding his thinking. It is a radical shift from the heretofore sensitive, genteel Frank Corsini.

Dr. Stenson called him at work to find out why his scheduled appointment was cancelled. Frank is now in full denial regarding the possibility of psychosis. He explains that he is very busy and he will reschedule as soon as possible. He abruptly ends the call.

Daily physical therapy consists of stretching, deep massage, electric stimulation, water therapy, strengthening exercises, and weight bearing. Wendy has developed Frank's regimen and guides him through the various phases. The eventual goals are to get him up and walking and to regain movement in his arm and hand.

Much to Sarah's chagrin, Wendy also assists with his showers and grooming. Frank has become sexually attracted to the young, pretty physical therapist. He has not had sex with his wife since he had the stroke. He never cheated on Sarah, although opportunities to do so have presented themselves on many occasions.

It is obvious to Wendy that she excites him, especially after his showers when she helps him dry off. His arousals, although only partial, are noticeable, because he has a very large penis—it is much larger than any man she ever dated. Frank has caught her glance at his groin in the past. Today while helping him dry off, he gently took her hand and placed it on his penis. She slowly strokes it and within seconds it reacted, getting longer and thicker. Wendy remarked, "Frank that thing is almost scary."

He places his right hand behind her head and pulls it down. She is holding his erect penis with both of her hands. She then directed the large bulbous-shaped head into her mouth. Frank continued gently pushing her head downward onto his penis—it was almost too thick for her mouth. Frank never cheated on his wife, because he had a low threshold for guilt. In the days and weeks to come, Wendy will sleep in Frank's bed every night and the outcries of passion during lovemaking will resonate throughout the large home during the early morning hours.

Frank calculates it will be impossible for Sarah not to know what's going on, and soon her lover will be too ill to satisfy her. The third member of their little cabal, Sam Goodman, may very well be a candidate for suicide.

With her self-esteem at low ebb, Sarah will spend her nights abusing martinis and lurking near her husband's bedroom listening to Wendy gasping and rocking the bed while on top of Frank. Sarah is on the verge of a nervous breakdown.

Chapter 16

IT'S ABOUT 5:30 AM WHEN FRANK'S THERAPIST INFORMS him that Barry was holding on his private line. When Frank picks up the phone, Barry states, "I received terrible news this morning. Sam committed suicide—he shot himself at home early this morning."

Barry informed Frank that Sam and Leda were in a lot of debt and Sam was also in some sort of trouble involving bribery. Barry asked, "Did you know anything about that?"

Frank responded, "Yes, but it's all moot now." He then asked Barry, "Who informed you about this unfortunate turn of events?"

"My doctor, Ira Slayman. I called him because my ulcers are acting up." Barry explained that they are bleeding and painful, but he's going to put off visiting with the doctor again unless they worsen.

Frank asks, "You coming over for cocktails tonight?"

"Yeah, but I'm not coming into the office today, I'll see you later."

At cocktail time, Barry announces that he needs to lay off the alcohol for a little while. Frank graciously volunteered to make him a chocolate milk shake and Barry accepted. So Frank hastily created a chocolate concoction garnished with

30 milligrams of Coumadin.

Sarah guzzled martinis until she fell asleep in her chair. While Frank and Wendy were sipping their wine, he asked Barry when the ulcers had started flaring up.

"Over a week ago," Barry said. He informed them that there was considerable bleeding, black stool, red blood discharge, and moderate-to-heavy pain.

Wendy suggested that he should see his doctor. Barry indicated that if the condition continued or worsened over the next few days, he would make an appointment with Dr. Slayman. Frank thought to himself, *He'll be in the hospital before the week is over.* Frank told Barry to take some time off.

The next morning Frank instructed his secretary to find out about Sam's wake and funeral arrangements. Then he called his Human Resources department and told the manager to contact one of the employment agencies that Windy City used regularly and get them started putting together a pool of architects for him to interview. Sam's position had to be filled immediately. He also instructed the Human Resources manager to contact the business departments of local universities and determine if there were any senior undergraduates available for an internship in Barry's sales division.

Frank's short-term strategies will set the stage for his visions and long-term plans, the crux of which is to turn Windy City over to his only child, Nick. However, several years will be required to formally educate, mentor, and finally to position Nick in the family enterprise. In the meantime, Frank is pleased with his decision to leave Nick at school in Europe. When Nick completes his studies in Italy, he will be enrolled a MBA program at one of the Ivy League schools. Nick is Frank's prince—he will inherit the Corsini monarchy.

Chapter 17

Sam's wake was a one-day affair and well-attended. Frank, assisted by Wendy, and Sarah arrived at about 6:00 pm. They made the appropriate rounds, expressing sympathy to Sam's family and reminiscing with friends. Sarah's speech was slurred and thick-tongued, so it was obvious that she had been drinking and Frank wanted people to see that.

He also made a point to speak with Dr. Ira Slayman. They talked about the problems that led Sam to taking his own life. The doctor asked Frank to elaborate about the bribery allegations, but Frank informed the doctor that he did not have any details about the situation. He feels that the less said about the matter, the better for the family. Dr. Slayman agreed and Frank shifted the conversation. He wanted the doctor to know that he was worried. "I love him like a brother, as I did Sam, but he's got to get treatment for those ulcers."

Dr. Slayman agreed, "I cannot force Barry to come into the office."

Frank replied, "Barry was here earlier, but he went home, because he was not feeling well."

The doctor cautioned, "He is running the risk of serious complications by delaying his treatment."

Having accomplished what he set out to do this evening, Frank located Sarah, said their goodbyes, and instructed Wendy to take them home. The instant they walked into the house, Sarah poured herself a gin-on-the-rocks. She started lamenting about poor Sam and his family. Then she addressed Frank directly and blubbered, "This is a huge loss to the company."

Frank and Wendy were sitting on a sofa together. He responded that losing Sam saddened him and he worried about Barry's illness, also. Frank said, "Windy City will survive." He followed up that conversation with recommending, "Sarah, you should seek help for your problem. Why don't you talk to Dr. Amber Wallace at my Rehab Center?"

Sarah was seated in an armchair across the room, sipping her gin and glaring at them. "I hope you don't think I'm blind, deaf, and stupid. I hear you fucking every night, all night."

Frank interrupted her, "Sarah, I do not believe this is a good time to discuss cheating ways. It would be a much more interesting and productive conversation, if Barry was here." Sarah sprang from her chair, threw her glass against the wall, and stormed out of the house.

Chapter 18

At about 4:00 am, Frank's phone awakens him. It's Sarah and she is in a panic, "Frank, I'm at Barry's place. He's terribly ill and can't get out of bed."

"Put him on the phone, Sarah,"

"He's in too much pain, he can't move."

Frank told Sarah to call 911, have Barry taken to the hospital, and most importantly, have the hospital notify Dr. Slayman. "Make sure they know he is Barry's doctor."

At about 3:00 pm that day, Frank contacted Dr. Slayman and inquired about Barry's status. The doctor told him Barry is not doing well, "He waited too long Frank." The doctor went on to explain that Barry is vomiting blood, and the pain is excruciating. Furthermore, there may be an infection that has formed in his gastrointestinal tract. "We believe he has a rare form of gangrene that progresses rapidly and has a high mortality rate." The doctor then reminded Frank about their conversation about the risks of delaying proper treatment.

Frank asked, "Doctor, are you saying that Barry could die from his ulcers?"

"Absolutely—but let's say ulcers and lifestyle."

Frank felt more confident than ever before about his course of action. In the state of Illinois, the fact that an attending physician will sign his patient's death certificate and suggest cause of death will usually preclude involvement by the medical examiner's office. There would not be an autopsy unless the police or family requested one. Barry had no wife or children, and what little family he did have all knew he suffered with ulcers for years. This is not a policy matter. Barry died within a very short period of time. Dr. Slayman recorded the cause of death as gas gangrene, complicated by liver damage and kidney failure.

Following Barry's funeral, Frank sat in his home study that evening sipping on a glass of wine and musing upon the events of the past few months. Barry and Sam were no longer consequential. Sarah who is tottering between insanity and a nervous breakdown agreed to see Dr. Amber Wallace for therapy.

One more detail needs his attention. He uses the house intercom to summon Wendy into the study. Over a glass of wine, he informed her that their affair must end and she has to move out. Wendy is stunned, but before she a chance to respond, Frank tells he that he is going to set her up and finance a physical therapy clinic that would be located in the new commercial plaza that Windy City was building.

Chapter 19

IT HAS BEEN SEVERAL WEEKS SINCE BARRY'S DEATH AND Sarah has been pouring her soul out to Dr. Amber Wallace. They discussed her long affair with Barry; her attempts to sway her husband's business decisions acting in concert with Barry and Sam; her alcoholism; and her bewilderment over Frank's personality transformation after the stroke.

With regard to the latter, Dr. Wallace consulted with Dr. Stenson to whom she had referred Frank, because of his work with NDE patients. He informed Amber that Frank abruptly withdrew from treatment, stating pressing business commitments as a reason.

Dr. Stenson's most recent work has been devoted to the study of NDEs and reincarnation. He set aside his psychotherapy practice in order to focus more on this research. However, he accepted Dr. Wallace's referral, because she was one of his favorite students and because Frank's case fell within the scope of his current studies.

The doctor recalls some of his dialogue with Frank regarding his management style. They had been discussing tenant evictions, the confiscation of property, and being hated. He remembered that something he had read for class reminded of Frank's comments. He began scanning the library in his home study and came upon a book containing the works of Niccolo Machiavelli, the great political philosopher of the Renaissance Period. He remembered now—Machiavelli's book, *The Prince*, was required reading in his business courses.

Machiavelli talked about surviving as a leader and rather than espousing lofty moral ideals, he concluded that virtues will result in a leader's destruction, whereas vices allow him to survive. Rather than have a reputation of being generous, it is best for a leader to have a reputation of being stingy. Frank informed the doctor that he always charged high rent and refused to waiver from his rates. In *The Prince*, Machiavelli indicates that it is better to be feared than loved. However, a leader must avoid being hated, which he can easily accomplish by not confiscating property.

Machiavelli also concluded in this work that a leader must be severe when punishing people, not merciful, and he must know how to be deceitful when it suits his purpose. Machiavelli praised Caesar Borgia, the much-despised tyrant of northern Italy during the fifteenth century, as the model Prince.

As tempting as it was to contemplate such a grand reincarnation, Dr. Stenson started to rationalize. We know for a fact that Frank went through a classic near death experience and has had a radical personality shift. He now shares similar values with a sixteenth century political philosopher. Frank's ancestors came here from Florence, Italy—Machiavelli was a Florentine.

In a rush of what Dr. Stenson believes to be reality, he thinks aloud, "All this does not make for a NDE Reincarnation yet." One of the most important tenets of the phenomenon he has been researching for the past several years is not present in the Frank Corsini case. Dark Energy is inexorably linked to a common progenitor, such as lineage. The doctor pours himself some brandy and sits in his favorite armchair. He begins reading more about Machiavelli, the Medici family, Caesar Borgia, and others of that time.

Just as drowsiness starts to set in, he reads something that causes him to become wide-eyed and abruptly sit up rigid, almost causing him to spill his brandy. He reads about Machiavelli, his many mistresses, and his distraught and jilted wife, *Marietta Corsini.*

Justice in this case was instigated by Hate, Rage, and Dark Energy.
Our Maker will administer Mr. Corsini's Justice!!!

SECTION III

The Pride of Rhoidsville

Chapter 1

The Pride of Rhoidsville
The Best and the Brightest

IT'S FAIR TO SAY THAT LAW ENFORCEMENT IN THIS COUNTRY has never been better. In the last fifty years, cops have done a relatively good job in building a reputation as professionals and an acceptable level of public trust. All of this is evidenced by the significant elevation of employment standards, the establishment of quality recruit training, and the placement of qualified people into leadership positions.

What you are about to read has nothing to do with quality policing—it's about counterfeit professionals created by political influence, patronage, and nepotism—you know, "The Divine Right."

The setting for this story could be any small- to medium-sized police department in any suburb, near any major city. For the sake of future reference, we need a name for the suburb we are looking at, so due to its anal political nature, we will call the place, "Rhoidsville." The town has been governed by the same mayor for over forty years, Major Eugene Holipski.

When a politician has been in power for such a long period of time, he or she is no longer a mere human—they are, especially in their own minds and word, omniscient—beyond mortal and bulletproof. Egoism is the order of the day.

Some of the characters in this story are detectives on the Rhoidsville Police Department, while others are descendants or hacks of "His Omniscience." Rhoidsville's detectives are pretty good actors. They talk and dress the part, they mimic big city investigators reasonably well in terms of jargon and fashions, but that's about as far as the comparison can be stretched. Whenever a major crime occurs in Rhoidsville, and thank God that's not often, the detectives there frantically reach out for help from the big city or neighboring suburbs. Most of the detective units in the towns nearby possess the skills, training, and resources needed to participate in major crime investigations. However, Rhoidsville has a problem. It's a matter of institutionalized cognition deficit manifested by domineering politics, or that which many people recognize as, "The Banana Republic syndrome," specifically characterized by very narrowly focused agendas.

In most law enforcement agencies, detectives are assigned or appointed from the rank and file by virtue of good past performance and achievements. In Rhoidsville the criteria for appointment is submissiveness, primal feebleminded loyalty to his omniscience and of course, pedigree. Now then, allow me to present to you, "The Best and the Brightest," the Rhoidsville detective unit.

Captain Stan Batko is boss of the detectives. He is also known as (aka) Captain Latex. The captain earned his aka as the result of a duty related action, which could have proven harmful to him. He uses an interrogation technique, specifically with male subjects, for which he is renowned. The boss has the suspect strip complete from the waist down, he then instructs them to bend over and grab their ankles. Usually most suspects believe that they are being strip-searched. The captain, now striking with the speed of a snake, grabs as much of the suspect's genitalia as possible and, while applying a vice-like grip, he begins yelling questions into the shocked arrestee's ear. He has to yell to be heard over the screams of the squirming suspect. Captain Batko has a powerful handgrip, because prior to this appointment to command the detective unit by his uncle, the mayor, he worked as a tombstone stacker in his father's monument factory, and as a gravedigger.

Now, let's talk about the captain's courageous, almost injurious event, which occurred during the interrogation of a Neanderthal-looking littering suspect whose screams were ear-shattering. The captain, always alert, realized that something was amiss. As it turned out, the arrestee was suffering from a severe case of gonorrhea, so the pressure from the grip on his scrotum caused a large quantity of morbid matter produced by the raging infection to pour bountifully into our hero's hand. Henceforth, before conducting his unique questioning technique, the captain now adorns his hands with latex surgical gloves.

Sgt. Thomas Reardon is also known as "Tommy Nice Guy." The origin of the detective's nickname is really self-explanatory. He's a nice guy, such a nice guy that he shares things with his colleagues—things he should not share. For example he announced to his co-workers he seldom has sex with his wife, Tina, because she doesn't want children yet. She has told Tommy that taking the pill could be dangerous, therefore, if she is willing to practice abstinence, so should he.

For your edification, Tina is the mayor's youngest of two daughters and the police department's animal warden, a position better known as dogcatcher.

Detective James Zizzo, aka "Jimmy Ding-Dong is married to Mayor Holipski's niece. The significance of his aka is the endowment of a ten-inch long, four-inch wide penis, which when limp swings to and fro like a pendulum bell. This super penis, along with ten pounds of balls has Jimmy thinking of himself as a centaur. By the way, he's harpooning Tommy Nice Guy's wife regularly. She's been on the pill for years and loves getting stuffed by "Ding-Dong."

Lastly, we have Detective Ted Bielecki, aka "Teddy Dis and Dat." This nickname relates to the way he talks, which is influenced by Polish/American vernacular. Teddy is Mayor Holipski's nephew, and Jimmy Ding-Dong's brother-in-law. He's a big guy, about six feet-five inches tall, weighs about 250 pounds. He has close-cropped, hedgerow-like hair, protruding ears, and a forehead like a tow-truck bumper. Teddy is certainly no slave to fashion—he wears the same old navy blue suit every day with a soiled white shirt and a 1950s vintage knit tie. He wears factory worker-style shoes with white socks. Teddy usually works with Ding-Dong, who finds him embarrassing and virtually not streetable. On occasion Jimmy will say something like, "Teddy, ya look like a homeless dumpster diver." Things that Teddy says in public are usually terribly embarrassing, also. Just the other day while having a cup of coffee in a crowded doughnut shop with Jimmy, he engaged in a conversation with other customers who were talking about the recent cold snap. He regaled them with the following bit of information, "Da udder day I was watching TV and dey said data small dog or an owl somewhere seen its shadow and dats why it's so cold—I tink it was called Pocahontas Pete or somting like dat." You can just imagine the eye rolling that was going on over that one.

To help you get a good picture or feel for the Rhoidsville detectives' office, I need to appeal to one of your five senses. The area is redolent with Teddy's aversion to showering on a regular basis, Jimmy's addiction to Italian cigars, Tommy's overuse of cheap after-shave lotion, and Captain Batko's incessantly neurotic use of various disinfectant sprays. It can get one's olfactory organ screaming!

At this point, if I have aroused your interest at all, you're probably wondering why I did not first introduce you to the chief of police. You see, whether figuratively or literally, whichever your imagination prefers, there is no chief. Rhoidsville is Mayor Holipski's town and there is no room or use for any other leader figures.

Whomever it was that said being omniscient was easy didn't know much. The mayor has to do it all, which includes running the town's departments. For mayors like Rhoidsville's, police departments represent their infantry and Mayor Holipski has staffed his well. His shaping of the department has, without a doubt, played key roles in the successes of his ambitions and visions. Just one example of such victories resulting from the mayor's wisdom and micromanagement are several lopsided defeats of attempts to unionize his police agency. Dealing directly with our own personally placed people is far more advantageous than having to do business with some chief, the chain of command, or God forbid, a union.

Chapter 2

The Spirit of Competition

SUBURBAN POLICE DEPARTMENTS ARE GENERALLY SIMILAR IN terms of size, structure, and degree of professionalism. The size of a suburban agency is usually based on the population of its service area. Structure is dependent on the work required, that is, are duties oriented towards traffic and routine calls for service or is the area plagued by high crime? Professionalism is evidenced by high employment standards, up-to-date management techniques, and state-of-the-art creative strategies.

Successful law enforcement agencies are those who employ quality recruiting and promotion processes and incorporate continuously elevating standards with extensive relevant testing. Typically well-managed departments, regardless of size, embrace a philosophy of stringent criteria along with comprehensive pre-employment examinations at the entry-level, and honest, fair, competitive testing for promotions.

Rhoidsville happens to be atypical—please remember that a Banana Republic strives to accomplish the status quo. Furthermore, intellect, honest competition, and level playing fields can be obstacles to business as usual in such an environment. Mayor Holipski, being the good politician, has been creative in his effort to avoid elitism on his police department. As he puts it, "Der ain't nutton worst dan a bunch a questions asken know-it-alls, hell, who knows what dey might be up to?"

The Mayor has personally appointed a three-person independent Civil Service Commission to conduct testing for hiring new officers and making promotions. The Mayor has publicly stated, "Ders no room in Rhoidsville for politics in da department, darefore I'm appointing tree people to keep tings squeaky clean." The appointees are three of the Mayor's precinct captains who know absolutely zero about police work, or management systems. Mayor Holipski has privately instructed his commission to be especially careful with "does overeducated collage bastards." In Rhoidsville, the term *overeducated* has been utilized when no other viable reason could be presented to eliminate candidates for employment. Another term frequently used is "overqualified."

Fortune has shown down on us, because we will be able to see Rhoidsville's civil service commission in action. They are in the midst of testing new officer applicants and police department candidates for promotion to sergeant. First let's take a closer look at the commission's methods.

With regard to new officer applicants, there is a four-step process, physical/psychological exams, background investigation, written test, and oral exam. Scoring is done as follows: physical/psychological exams and background investigation are pass/fail. The written test makes up for 40 percent of the applicant's final score, the oral example exam accounts for 60 percent of the final score. Scores of less than 70 percent on either the written or the oral exams mean, without exception, failure and thus exclusion from any eligibility list. Sounds simple enough, does it not?

First of all, the pass/fail parts of this process are a no-brainer, fail the physical/psychological or background check and you're gone. Now, just for the sake of understanding, let's look at a hypothetical case score: If an applicant's written test score is 80, the process conversion value is 32. Let's assume the applicant's oral exam score is 80, the conversion value is 48. The applicant's final score in this hypothetical example is 80, 48+32=80. Easy? Maybe?

Here is the commission's testing process for promotion to sergeant: There are three phases, the written exam having a value of 20%, the oral example has a value of 16 percent. The performance evaluation is conducted by the mayor himself.

Indeed, this is a process that should satisfy even the most skeptical of observers. The written exams for both the entry level and promotion tests are administered and scored by a private firm at great taxpayer expense. However, it's worth it according to Mayor Holipski because, it avoids hanky-panky!

The oral exams are conducted and scored by the Civil Service Commission. Rest assured that the mayor has picked the most agreeable and loyal precinct captains for this task. The past performance evaluation, which is only part of the process, is conducted by the mayor's office, with consultation of Captain Batko. Why does the mayor's office conduct the past performance evaluations? Well, you see, the mayor's been around long enough to know his people and how they perform. One cannot question the knowledge and wisdom of "His Omniscience," —anyway, no one has ever complained!

Fifty people have applied for the position of new officer. The requirements to participate in the testing process are: the applicant must be between the ages of 21 and 35; possess a high school diploma or its equivalency; be of good character and moral turpitude; possess a driver's license; and sign an agreement that states that the applicant understands that he or she cannot review or appeal test results.

The commissioners have assured one and all that there will be absolutely no exceptions to the rules of the Civil Service Commission. One of the fifty applicants for new officer is Mayor Holipski's eldest of two daughters, Marylin Dumphries, a 37-year-old divorcee. She works for the police department in a civilian capacity, i.e., a records clerk, and has been so employed for the past three months. The Civil Service Commission has indicated that her position as a records clerk exempts her from any age restriction. Marylin is a stout woman, about five feet two inches tall, and weighs approximately 225 pounds, give or take 10 pounds. Her complexion has a hue similar to radish skin. The civil service commission has further announced that Marylin's position with the city also exempts her from the physical and psychological exam requirements. In any other jurisdiction, this would certainly raise questions by the pension board, which must approve all new officers' participation in the pension fund.

Mayor Holipski, leaving no political stone unturned, has judiciously appointed loyalists to the police department pension board. With reference to the test for new officers that just took place, 49 of the 50 applicants passed the written test with scores of 70 or higher. The group average was 75, the highest score was 85, the lowest was a failing score of 45. By the way, the applicant who failed? You guessed it, radish-face Marylin.

The commission, now confronted with a new mission, must conduct an emergency meeting. These hacks are so into the commission bullshit, they wear police uniforms for their meetings—that's right, 60- and 70-year-old morons playing cops. In addition, these costumes are adorned with Rhoidsville police badges and shoulder patches. Each commissioner also wears collar insignia pins, for example, Commissioner Ryan has lieutenants bars on his collars; Commission Zucas has captains bars on each collar, while Commission Chairman Randazzo has four general stars on one collar, and a full bird-colonel pin on the other. Apparently he doesn't know what he wants to be. Seeing these buffoons in action is funnier than watching a monkey fuck a football, and all of this at taxpayers' expense. Their emergency meeting went something like this:

Chairman Randazzo, "Da special meetin of da Rhoidsville Civil Service Commission is now started, hey you guys wanna go to Scardina's afder for pizza?"

Commissioner Zucas: "Pizza sounds OK to me, I make whachacall it, you know motion dat dis commission lower da police written test score for passing from 70 to 45."

Commissioner Ryan: "Me to, I mean I second dat, and I radar have pasta dan pizza."

Chairman Randazzo: "All in favor of da score ting say yeah.

I think you get the picture.

The rest of the testing process went as follows:

None of the applicants, except Marylin, were given a score higher than 70 by the commissioners on the oral exam. Marylin's score was 100. Here's how it all broke down, Marylin's written test score was 45, this amounted to a conversion score of 18 (40% of 45=18). Her oral interview score was 100; this converted to 60 (60% of 100=60). Marilyn's final score: 78 (18+60).

The applicant who scored highest on the written, was a 25-year-old recent college graduate, he scored 85, therefore, (40% of 85 = 34) his score of 70 on the oral converted to a 42. Final score: 76 (34+42).

Voila! Another job well done by your civil service commission, nobody failed, all of the applicants made the eligibility list, and as usual cream always rises to the top.

Now let's look at the test for promotion to sergeant. Only 10 cops out of 30 patrol officers and detectives are participating. It's apparent that two-thirds of Rhoidsville's officers cannot deal with hard-nosed, straight-up competition, even though several of them are college graduates.

The front-runner is Detective Thomas Reardon, Mayor Holipski's son-in-law. Although Tommy has never been to college, he did spend a few weeks in culinary school at the local YMCA. The mayor has quietly predicted a Reardon victory. Tommy's past performance evaluation will show that his greatest attribute is one that Captain Batko and Mayor Holipski consider the most important, that is, blind loyalty. Now don't forget there are three phases to the Civil Service Commission's promotion test: the written exam with the value of 25 percent and the past performance evaluation of the value of 50 percent.

All test results are in, the group average on the written exam was 78, with two candidates scoring in the 90s, and the highest score was 92. By the way, the two cops who scored in the 90s are considered to be nosey up-starts, you know the type, always with the questions, especially the most irritating question of all, "WHY?"

With the exception of Tommy Reardon, nobody scored higher than 70 on the orals or past performance evaluation. The results of Tommy's test went as follows: he scored 70 on the written exam, which converted to 17.5; he scored 100 on the oral interview which converted to 25; his past performance evaluation score was 100, which converted to 50. Final score: 92.5 (17.5+25+50=92.5).

The cop who scored 92 on the written had a final score of 78 (43+17.5+17.5=78).

Again, nobody failed and superior intellect was the order of the day. Another one of the mayor's predictions has come to pass, he is truly all-knowing.

I'll bet you doubting Thomases are thinking that Marylin will never make it through the police academy—sorry, guess again. Police department records will show that she breezed right on through to certification.

She will serve on the department for two years and then petition the pension board for a disability pension, due to a duly related illness, that is, hypertension and obesity. The pension board will vote to give her the lifelong pension. All at taxpayer expense!

Chapter 3

They Never Touched Dessert

THE MID-NOVEMBER SNOW MADE FOR A BEAUTIFUL Thanksgiving landscape and provided the kickoff for a vivacious Christmas spirit. For the past three years the detective unit has thrown a private Christmas party at various restaurants in town. Due to the nature of things in Rhoidsville, this annual celebration is usually complementary. Unlike most American law enforcement agencies, the Rhoidsville PD is not adverse to or uncomfortable with gratuitous merchants, especially restaurants and taverns. The Rhoidsville detectives' Christmas merrymaking has been comped 100 Percent. That's really good considering these festivals were literally food and liquor bazaars. Restaurant owners have been astonished by the eating and drinking capacity of only four mirthful, frolicsome cops. This year the boys had decided to go Italian, at Scardina's Restaurant and Bar. The captain has instructed Jimmy Zizzo to make the arrangements with the owner, Ugo Scardina. Ugo is Sicilian-born and has been in the country for thirty years or so. He is in his early 60s, chubby and balding, and somewhat swarthy-looking.

Scardina's is your typical Italian American eatery—each table is covered with checkered red and white fabric and equipped with glass shakers of grated cheese, Italian seasonings, a narrow-stemmed bottle containing olive oil, and a mug with several bread sticks. Mr. Scardina has taken Jimmy's reservation and assured him everything will be fine. The boys will be served family style. The Rhoidsville detectives have been helpful to the restauranteur, especially last year when the parents of Rosa, a short 16-year-old porker who is one of Ugo's dishwashers, complained to police that Rosa and Ugo were having an affair. The issue was even stickier than the parents knew, because unbeknownst to them was the fact that Ugo had knocked Rosa up, she was about two months gone. The captain and his unit were extremely responsive—they kept Rosa's parents in the dark, and referred the lovers to an abortion clinic in the city. Afterwards Ugo always comped the boys when they stopped in his bar for some cocktails, but they had never eaten there and it was time to cash in. The party was set for a Friday night in mid-December.

On the night of the party when two of the boys arrived at about 6:30, the place was packed with paying customers. In attendance was the captain, Jimmy, Teddy, and Tommy. Once they were formally greeted by Ugo and settled in, the first of many entrées was served up, a huge, table-sized, antipasto, a half a dozen baskets of garlic French bread, and about one gallon of Chianti wine. The partiers engaged the food and drink like men who were going to jail tomorrow. They went through the oversized antipasto like piranha on a feeding frenzy, but it was the sounds flowing from their table that held patrons and staff in awe. Perhaps the best analogy one can offer is the sounds emanating from a group of famished boars—wine was being chugged by the water glass full. Ugo and his staff quickly realized that keeping up with this hog show would be tough sledding, Well, what the hell, when one doesn't have to worry about money, moderation, and restraint, it gives way to shamelessness.

Two extra-large antipasto platters and two gallons of wine, later the second entrée was served family style. Three large platters of ravioli were put on the table, with more garlic bread and two more gallons of Chianti. Teddy asked the waiter for beer mugs to drink the wine with. The waiter returned to the table with four beer mugs and there for his wondering eyes to behold laid the platters, empty, and the fellas were clamoring for more. Ugo passed by just in time to see the captain hold his plate in the air with both hands, tilt it toward his face and let several ravioli slide into his mouth. Teddy thought that was cool, so he tried it, but because he was a bit too tipsy, ravioli ended up all over his face and lap. The waiter returned to the table with three more platters of ravioli to the cheers of Rhoidsville's best and brightest. The gluttony continued until around midnight. Five or six gallons of wine had passed over the lips of Captain Batko and his boys, along with unimaginable quantities of food, so now it was time for dessert.

Ugo walked to the table with a tray of sweets and with subtle Sicilian cunning set the tone of the festivities for the remainder of the night when he announced, "My friends, the sweet tray is on me," and simultaneously he quickly slipped an inebriated Jimmy Zizzo the bill. Walking away backwards, so as to keep facing the mirth-makers, he exclaimed, "Please, please enjoy."

The tab total was $540. Captain Batko snatched the tab from Jimmy's hand, and upon scrutinizing it, he bellowed through a thick wine-soaked tongue, "A bit pricey, ain't it?" The captain now looking around the table at his droopy-eyed, red faced team, stated, "I think dis guy tinks he's cute and we're dummies … when I'm tru wit dis Dago bastard, he'll tink twice about screwing wit us again." At this point Tommy who is really a nice guy and not much of a drinker started burping up—vurping is a better description. Teddy, with blood shot, glassed-over eyes, looked at the bill; he tried to say something but instead he puked all over himself. When Tommy saw Teddy let go, his vurping quickly escalated upwards and outwards. The food and drink, mixed with the issue of Ugo's bill, was having more of a laxative effect on Jimmy.

The captain continued to rant and rave incoherently about the thought of paying for something. His rage and wine swilling caused his tongue and mucus membrane to thicken, resulting in laryngitis. The sight of all of this left Ugo's staff, especially the cleanup crew, speechless.

After finally coming up with the money to cover the bill, the captain and his men made their way from the table, slipping and sliding and trying to maintain equilibrium. It is easy to understand that at this point, balance is far more important than dignity. Upon leaving the restaurant, Captain Batko was heard to say in a choking, strained voice, "Da Mayor's gonna hear about da shit we had to put up wit tonight." An unconcerned Ugo, who is a heavy contributor to Mayor Holipski's campaign fund yelled out to the crew, "Have a great holiday, guys."

On his way home, the captain decided to stop in at the department and have a few coffees—he did not want to go home totally shit-faced. He was still fuming over the audacity of Ugo Scardina—what insolence. The captain asked himself, "Is dis guy shameless … or what?" As he entered the interior offices of the department, he noticed an officer talking to a young girl, who was seated at a desk in the interview room. The girl was obviously upset and her clothing was in disarray.

When the officer, a young rookie, saw the captain looking into the interview room, he rose from his desk and approached him, but not out of earshot of the girl. The captain asked, "What ya got, kid?"

"Sir, this girl claims a guy tried to rape her tonight."

The captain asked, "Is she local?" "No, sir, she lives in the city." "Dat figures," said the boss. With his face still red from the Chianti, the boss asked," Have you done a face composite yet?"

"No sir," he replied.

"I'll do dat for you, kid." The captain walked into the office, sat at the desk, and with that husky, deeper than normal, voice introduced himself, "Hi, dare, I'm Captain Batko, Chief of da Detectives." His speech was still somewhat slurry, and his breath added to the young girl's tear production. A face composite is actually a computerized program used by investigators to build a facial likeness of a suspect. The program software contains photos of hundreds of chin line, eyebrows, eyes, noses, ears, and lips. With the guidance of a good investigator, the witness or victim chooses facial features that most resemble those of the suspect, until with some luck, an entire facial likeness is produced.

The captain's bad breath, thick-tongued speech, and general demeanor were obviously making the young victim more uncomfortable. His opening question set the tone for the remainder of the interview, "Was dis guy white or a nigger, darling?" As the captain fumbled with the computer keyboard and mouse, surprisingly a facial image began to emerge, then he exclaimed, "Good, we're done—how's dat little lady?"

He handed her a printout, she looked at it, looked at the captain, turned to the young officer and said, "Please, I want to go home." She appeared to be terrified.

The captain, now with his eyelids drooping over his badly bloodshot eyes said, "Sure little girl, you can go home and rest easy cause we're gonna get dis creep."

The captain handed the rookie the facial image printout and commented, "Here you go, kid, it's easy when ya know what you're doin'." The officer looked at the printout, his mouth dropped open, and he took two steps backward—the facial image had no nose.

Chapter 4

Rhoidsville Heroics

MANY SUBURBS HAVE SUCCESSFUL GOVERNMENTS, BECAUSE their revenue base is supported by the taxation of commercial enterprises, especially large shopping centers. Taxes levied on retail sales can represent a significant portion of a town's revenue. Suburbs with multiple, colossal malls have literally become tax fat.

So it goes with Rhoidsville, a town with a residential population of about 25,000 and an average transient population of approximately half a million people per day. This non-permanent population is made up of people who work in Rhoidsville's commercial and industrial centers, and shoppers who spend considerable time and money at its six large malls and gallerias.

Rhoidsville's residents are predominantly senior citizens, about 60 percent are over 60 years of age. Mayor Holipski likes it that way. Old people seldom cause major problems and, more importantly, they prefer the status quo. They are relatively dependent on government and they never run for elected positions. The mayor has run unopposed for his last four terms. All of this plays well with the internal and external circumstances of a Banana Republic.

By the way, Rhoidsville is lily-white, and the seniors like

that, because you see anything out of the ordinary—I should say their ordinary, such as Mexican landscapers and black delivery people—alarm Mayor Holipski's over-65 block.

The mayor is very responsive to his senior constituents. After all, they represent about 15,000 loyal votes. Furthermore, their concerns are usually singular and not complicated. A case in point occurred not too long ago when members of the mayor's Senior Citizens for Neighborhood Safety Association expressed concern about black mail carriers. The mayor ordered Captain Batko to look into and report on this potentially dangerous situation.

After discovering that the postmaster was a white man, the captain made an appointment with him. They met at the Post Office. Upon slapping his badge case down on the postmaster's desk, the captain announced, "Hi, I'm Captain Stan Batko, boss of da detectives."

The postmaster responded, "Hi, I'm Rich Kozak," he offered to the captain who, of course, applied a firm, manly handclasp.

The captain asked, "Rich, dat name Kozak, dats Polish, ain't it?"

"Yes, it is, captain."

"Hey, Richie, how come you got so many darkies delivering mail here? Da guy delivering in my neighborhood is a nigger."

"Captain, I don't know what to say. Are they doing anything wrong?"

"Dats da problem question, Richie, who knows … do you guys check dem out before you put dem on da job?"

Becoming more uncomfortable by the second, the postmaster responds, "What do you mean, captain?"

"Do you do a background investigation on dem … I mean, da guy you got in my neighborhood looks shifty."

"I believe there is some sort of background inquiry conducted, captain, but I'll ask you again, is there a report of any of my carriers doing something wrong?"

"Richie, I'll bet you dat dey all got a sheet. Give me da name and da date of birt on da one in my neighborhood. I'll run a check on him for you, OK?"

"Captain, I don't know if I can do that. Let me check with the Postal Inspector's office."

"Richie, we're bote Pollacks here. I can do dis ting on da QT."

"Captain, without authorization from the postal inspector, I don't think I can help you."

The captain, with his eyes bulging and jaw locked responds, "Pal, if anything happens to anybody at da hands of one of your niggers, it's on your head, do you understand dat?"

The postmaster looks the captain directly in the eyes and responds, "Gotch ya."

When Captain Batko reported to the mayor the outcome of his meeting with the postmaster, the mayor was furious, "Who da fuck does dat guy tink he is … you tell your cops to start working does shines over, understand?"

The captain instructed the patrol division commander to start questioning black mail carriers regarding their names and dates of birth. With this information, the police department could run criminal history background inquiries. The patrol officers and their supervisors, most of whom are dedicated to the law enforcement profession reluctantly complied with the captain's order. The black mail carriers, none of which by the way had ever been convicted of a crime, had nothing to hide, so they complied.

The aura of compliance exhibited by the Rhoidsville patrol officers ended abruptly during the height of the Christmas shopping season. Mayor Holipski received reports from his inner circle of imbeciles that local shoppers were becoming uncomfortable in some of Rhoidsville's shopping centers due to the increased presence of minorities and immigrants, especially blacks. The mayor met with Captain Batko and read him the riot act about tax revenue and the adverse impact that blacks are having on sales in the shopping malls.

Captain Batko told the patrol division commander to place his officers on walking beats in the shopping centers and harass blacks. As the harassment order passed down through the chain of command, its indecency generated serious questions upwards through the same chain of command. The division commander informed Captain Batko that a couple of young street sergeants were questioning the legality of the captain's order. When the captain was told who the sergeants were, he bellowed, "Send does two collage assholes into my office, NOW … I'll show you how to control dem."

The sergeants reported immediately, "What's up wit you two, what's your problem?" One of the sergeants spoke, "Sir, with all due respect, your order to harass minorities in our malls is de facto discrimination."

With the veins in his neck bulging, the captain shouts, "What in da fuck are you talking about wit dis de-facto shit."

The second young sergeant speaks up, "Sir, your order is blatantly illegal, and you cannot do this."

"Don't tell me what I can't do, you uppity asshole! What are you two—nigger lovers?

The sergeant who first spoke responds, "Sir, we are professional law enforcement officers …"

The captain cuts the sergeant off, "You'll do what I tell you to do, no questions asked. Now get out dare and do your job."

The same sergeant responds, "Sir, we will not obey any unlawful order, nor will we order our people to do so. What you are ordering will cause this agency to implode as a result of civil suits and probably criminal charges."

"You two are on suspension—two smart-ass bastards—GET OUT, GET OUT!"

Captain Batko now summons his detectives and orders them to "Get into does shopping centers and bust some shine balls."

That very evening, Sergeant Tommy Reardon, while in plain clothes and walking through a mall with a security officer, observed a young 13-year-old black kid walking into a clothing store. The kid was wearing an old army field jacket, which was much too big for him and had a first infantry division shoulder patch.

Tommy tells the security guard, "Watch how I handle this, because this is what we want mall security to do." Tommy approached the youngster and said, "Take the jacket off, gang banger." Keep in mind that Tommy has always been a nice guy, good hard-working parents raised him, and he never did anything to break their hearts.

Additionally, being a bully or better yet a street fighter was out of character for Tommy Reardon. The 13-year-old asked, "Who are you?"

Tommy displayed his badge and said, "Detective Thomas Reardon, you little shit. Now take the jacket off."

"Officer, this is my dad's jacket." Later it was learned that the boy's dad had served in the First Division (The Big Red One) in Vietnam, and was awarded a purple heart. When the kid told Tommy the jacket belonged to his dad, Tommy slapped him and tried to rip the jacket off.

The young boy was not big in stature, but having been raised in the inner city, he had the heart of a wolf. He countered Tommy's slap and attempt to remove the jacket with a solid left to the detective's lower abdomen, the area between the belt line and groin. Out of breath, Tommy tried to grab onto the youngster, but a mix of anger and fear fueled the boy. He caught Tommy with a combination of four quick overhand lefts and rights to the face.

The debacle started to draw a sizable crowd, who believed they were watching a mall promotion, because it made no sense that a small boy could pull off such a one-sided beating on a grown man.

Tommy, in desperation, started yelling to the security guard and the crowd, "Somebody help me with this nigger." One of the people in the crowd was the chairperson of a big city Democratic Rainbow Coalition, and he was in the company of an attorney for the American Civil Liberties Union.

The humiliation surrounding this episode and the civil suits that followed took their toll on Tommy's health. When Mayor Holipski publicly denounced Tommy's actions as racist and unauthorized, he suffered a minor stroke. Rhoidsville settled with the 13-year-old for about $250,000. Tommy had to spend two months in the hospital and he was put on Coumadin, a blood thinner.

His wife, Tina, who is Mayor Holipski's youngest of two daughters and the police department's dogcatcher, is also feeling humiliated because of Tommy's ass whipping at the hands of a 13-year-old black kid. She wants to leave him, but the Mayor has advised Tina that leaving her husband at this particular time is ill-advised, because due to his recent stroke, a divorce proceeding could have an unfavorable outcome for her and bad press for the Mayor. Her father, the Mayor, informed Tina, "Hold off for a while, honey. Maybe de dumb asshole will drop dead or get himself killed. You can't forget about da pension, baby doll."

Chapter 5

"Lips That Touch Liquor ..."

Politicians get an enormous amount of free publicity and photo-ops when they engage in "crackdowns." Ideally these tactics are intended to produce corrective action. Some of the most popular targets for crackdowns include, brothels, certain traffic offenses, and liquor related violations.

Rhoidsville's crackdowns add another dimension to this tactical strategy, that is, economics. In addition to its vast private business sector of shopping malls, filled with stores selling dry goods, food, electronics, information technology, and hardware, Rhoidsville has issued 85 liquor licenses. Mayor Holipski is also the town's liquor commissioner, so he has the final word on who can get a license to sell booze.

Now, of course, you realize that fees associated with such privileges, depending on the proposed establishment's location, size, and type of operation, can be exorbitant, even downright extravagant, and I hasten to add, out of the realm of usual and proper. The revenue realized from liquor license fees are usually divided two ways, part to the jurisdiction that issued the license and part to the State's Department of Revenue. If you have not already guessed it, you can rest assured that in Rhoidsville liquor license fees are apportioned differently. It's likened more to plundering with the liquor commissioner getting more than a fair share.

Another factor that did not escape the all-knowing, ever visionary mayor regarding business is the fact that every liquor establishment needs to have some liability insurance. In many jurisdictions, this coverage is called Dram-Shop insurance. This is the insurance that covers a liquor licensee being sued for directly or indirectly overserving, or illegally selling liquor to a person who has injured himself or another due to drinking too much. The mayor is partner in an insurance company that sells this type of coverage. His partner is Ruben Goldstein, an old-time big city lawyer. Incidentally, every one of Rhoidsville's liquor establishments, except one, is insured by the Integrity First Corporation.

Integrity First is a multidimensional enterprise that sells all types of insurance, management consultation, private investigations, brokers real estate, and lastly it is an ambulance-chasing law firm. With some legal razzle-dazzle Rube has been able to keep his partner's status in the corporation "silent." But it hasn't been easy, because the mayor wants to be known as the Alpha Dog, the preeminent leader, or as his dupes put it, "the go to guy."

If we were not talking about Rhoidsville, we would no doubt be discussing the law and such matters as official misconduct, conflict of interest, abuse of authority, etc., etc., ad infinitum. However, to Mayor Holipski, such issues are irrelevant—he has been around forever and considers himself bulletproof. His objective now is to maximize profits and minimize outlay with little, if any, concern for semblance.

It was mentioned earlier that Integrity First has insured all Rhoidsville's liquor establishments save one. Not insuring this joint, "The Greek Isles," was just another example of the mayor's omniscience. His infinitely keen perception enabled him to peg the place as a bad risk and thus he declined to insure it. A short time after opening, the place burned to the ground and it cost the company that did insure it well in excess of a million dollars.

The Rhoidsville Police found no evidence of arson. The state arson investigators and the crime lab were told by Captain Batko that their services were not required. The mayor is not only a consummate elected leader, he is also a businessman with keen insight. This sagaciousness has been exemplified time and again with his artfully sly use of "The Crackdown."

A short time ago he ordered his police detectives to crack down on hookers. "Get them bum bitches off da street and into da taverns where dey belong." Don't forget Dram Shop insurance policy premiums and business license fees are based on volume, so moving the hookers into the taverns increases volume. The mayor also wants his detectives doing regular random tavern checks to make sure that there is no one overserving minors. He has repeatedly told Captain Batko, "If one of does morons beats da shit out of a hooker or gets into a bad accident, I might have to pay a hefty claim."

While he was on this roll, the mayor continued, "By da way, Rube and me want copies of every DUI arrest and accident wit injuries dats reported to you people."

Now here is another stroke of genius. People arrested for DUI or are injured in an incident the proximate cause of which was alcohol intoxication need legal representation. Integrity First has every based covered. First, there is the inside track to the clients vis-à-vis police reports. Secondly, Rube or one of his referrals can probably exert considerable influence over a client who wants to sue an establishment insured by Integrity First. Lastly, and ultimately, the coup-de-grace is Integrity First Corporation's 90 percent acquittal rate in DUI cases. Uppity, righteous bastards arrested the ten percent that are not found innocent have no ambition for upward movement and no political acumen.

Just last year one of those young, righteous, college bastards arrested a client and longtime friend of the mayor and Rube. The arrestee, Al Stein, a 55-year old bookie, was involved in an accident. He rear-ended an old lady while traveling at high-speed. She was injured seriously and both cars were totaled. Al was not hurt, and he was charged wit DUI. He was so drunk that he acquiesced to a blood test. Blood was drawn at the hospital and the officer submitted it to the crime lab for analysis. Al had been drinking in a Rhoidsville tavern all day.

As soon as the mayor and Rube obtained all the police reports, representation of the old lady regarding a possible civil suit was referred to a local swindler frequently used by Integrity First. Rube wanted to personally defend his old buddy.

As the first court date for Al's DUI charge approached,

Captain Batko talked to the arresting officer, "Hey, kid, how's about helping out on da Stein DUI."

"In what way Captain? The lab results were conclusive that the guy was very drunk."

"Yeah, yeah, I know all dat … how's about you lose da lab report?"

"Captain, with all due respect and concern for that injured old lady, I cannot do that."

Back at the mayor's office, "Why do you keep hiring does collage assholes? Now you can figure out how to snatch dat lab report, Batko."

On the first court date, the officer obtained his case files from the records section and discovered that the crime lab report was missing from the Stein case folder. He informed the records director of the situation, but the director, never looking up from his desk said, "Please don't get me involved in this crap."

In court, the officer and the prosecutor asked for a continuance. The officer informed the judge that the lab report had not been received yet. Rube demanded to go to trial and he objected strongly to a continuance, "Your honor, the defense is ready for trial now!" The judge reluctantly granted a one-month continuance on the motion of the state.

The officer contacted the crime lab and instructed them to send another report to Rhoidsville, he also asked the lab to send a duplicate report to a colleague in a neighboring suburban policed department. On the next court date, the officer obtained the duplicate report from his pal. Upon obtaining the court case folder from the records section of his own department, he discovered the lab report was missing again. The records director smiled at the officer and said, "When are you new guys gonna learn."

When the officer walked into court, Rube and his client were grinning like chimpanzees. The judge opened the Stein case by asking the officer if he was successful in obtaining the lab report. The officer responded, "I was, Your Honor," while holding the report up for all to see.

Rube, now wide-eyed and speaking through clinched teeth, asked the judge for a sidebar with the prosecution. The judge responded, "Council, last time you insisted on going to trial, so let's get it on."

In a low voice Rube asked, "Your honor, the defense is requesting a side-bar." The judge passed the case for a short prosecution/defense conference. At the sidebar Rube asked the officer, "What are you, some kind of asshole?"

The officer sprang to his feet, "How about I flatten that hook nose of yours, you phony?" The prosecutor intervened immediately and restored order. At trial it was agreed that Al would plead guilty in exchange for no jail time, a $2,000 fine, and three years of probation.

Later that day the mayor told Rube, "We'll always have dat ten-percent of fucken do-gooders dat we got to work around, Rube." In the end, Integrity First made well over $15,000 in legal fees from Al, and indirectly the old lady. The attorney that represented the injured woman influenced her to decline suing the Rhoidsville Tavern insured by Integrity First. Al Stein's auto insurance company had to settle with her. The arresting officer is being labeled by Captain Batko and company as a cop who has no people skills.

By the way, that tavern where Al got drunk had its insurance premium increased by 15 percent.

Chapter 6

Merlin Would Be Envious

MERLIN THE MAGICIAN WHO BUILT THE ROUND TABLE FOR King Arthur during the Arthurian cycle in medieval times would relinquish his wand, if he had to compete with the magic carried out by Holipskian Cronies in Neo-Medieval Rhoidsville.

As you know, the mayor is extremely responsive to his senior citizen population. His administration supports several senior associations, such as, Senior Citizens for Neighborhood Safety; Senior Citizens for Open and Ethical Government; and others. Rhoidsville also provides programs for its over 60-year-old seniors, such as, free hot dog day, voter assistance, bingo, blood pressure testing, voter assistance, cooking lessons, more voter assistance, and pocket pool.

The mayor has been informed that the center needs two new pool tables and some accessories, the cost of which is approximately $2,100. Mayor Holipski has ordered some of his precinct captains and doorbell ringers to organize a fund-raiser. Rhoidsville is practically a patentee with a fund-raising episode they call a "Smoker." For all intents and purposes a more accurate title for this thing should be, "Smoker and Mirror." You are truly fortunate, because I can provide you with the mechanics of Rhoidsville's most recent fund-raising Smoker experience.

The Smoker in Rhoidsville is not an intricate affair. Complexity and potential entanglements are non-existent, because general accounting practices are avoided. Please remember the mayor's word is sacrosanct and it transcends accounting. The Smoker method of operation begins with the printing of admission tickets, which entitles the holder to a steak dinner and a chance to take part in a $5,000 grand prize raffle. Only 150 tickets are sold at a cost of $125 each. The concept here is that by limiting the number of tickets sold, the odds or winning are enhanced.

The smoker is a man's only party, because after dinner and the grand prize raffle, tables are cleared and the guys get down to some serious poker and they don't need a bunch of nagging , cackling, chatting broads around. The fund-raiser is always held at a Rhoidsville restaurant or banquet hall, because you never know when someone might get the idea that illegal gambling is going on. Many of the smoker tickets are purchased by local businesspeople that want to support worthwhile programs. Many of these busy folks will not attend and this allows smoker organizers to comp certain individuals. Got any ideas who might get comped? No, silly, not some senior citizen. Let me give you a hint to this rhetorical question, "Have you ever known a politician who will dig into his or her own pocket for anything?"

Here is how this fund-raiser would play out, if arithmetic were a factor: 150 tickets at $125 each comes out to $18,750. Expenses include: printing of 150 tickets, the meal ($1500), and the grand prize in the amount of $5,000.

A whopping $2,100 was proudly presented to the senior center by Mayor Holipski himself. Some of you may be thinking, "Hey, wait a minute, something isn't right." All I can say is be careful, because about five years ago a curious individual who was troubled by the amount of money awarded to his program from smoker funds stated, "What's happening with this thing makes no sense, you organizers are like fiduciaries." The mayor was at this meeting and with his eyes bulging and the veins in his neck protruding exclaimed, "Hey, pal, are you questioning our honesty—who da fuck do you tink you are, you ungrateful bastard, and anodder ting, swearing and name calling has no place here." The intrepid gentleman was given a vicious browbeating by the mayor and his band of hocus-pocus party makers.

In this most recent fund-raiser, the seniors accepted the money humbly and thanked the mayor and his organization at a photo-op. In case you're curious about who won the grand prize of $5,000, a close associate of the Integrity First Corporation, possessed the winning ticket.

Chapter 7

The Doberman Dare

RHOIDSVILLE'S ANIMAL WARDEN IS TINA REARDON, SHE IS the younger of Mayor Holipski's two daughters, and she is married to Sergeant Tommy Reardon. Tina is 30-years-old and she's a little on the chunky side, but nevertheless somewhat attractive. She has a pretty face, a big rack of tits, and a nice round, chubby ass.

You would think that as the police department's dogcatcher she appreciates dogs, cats, etc. Well, forget that notion, she finds animals downright disgusting. The only reason she made her father give her the job is so she could be close to all those cute cops.

Tina and Tommy have been married for about five years. Tommy is a pleasant guy, but she finds him boring, wimpy, and a piss-poor lover. They have very little in common: Tommy is nice, she's selfish and condescending; he's a home body, Tina likes to party—she loves to suck and fuck.

Tommy can take it or leave it and because he cannot satisfy her, he would sooner leave it. The fact that Tommy does not like to party doesn't slow her down one bit. Tina has an interesting personal doctrine: she believes that her one-night stands, which occur frequently, are indicative of a great lover. She is a woman who is capable of multiple organisms and her husband seldom gives her any. On more than a few occasion, she has had to finish herself off after having sex with him.

Another source of resentment for Tina is a social paradigm: when a married woman gets a little on the side, she's proclaimed a slut, but when a man does it, he's considered a stud. It's important for you to understand that Tina prides herself in the fact that she's a swallower. She claims that only one woman in every thousand goes south on a man, let alone swallows. "I'm one in a thousand," she proudly exclaims in local taverns and nightspots. In spite of the fact that she loves to suck and fuck, she has cut Tommy off, because, she has lost respect for him ever since a "little nigger" kicked his ass, and she goes on to tell friends that due to his weak character, he suffered a stroke. Tina cannot accept weakness in any man, whether it's caused by what she perceives to be cowardice or physical illness, it's all the same to her. When talking to her friends about Tommy, Tina uses terms such as coward, weakling, and sickly, but the major reason for her punishment of the man is because he is a bum fuck.

Tina's favorite piece of ass is Jimmy, Ding Dong, Zizzo. She has told friends, "When Jimmy fucks you with that ding-dong dick of his, you stay fucked. He's got ten pounds of balls that pommel my ass when he does me missionary. Just thinking and talking about him give me a warm, moist feeling downstairs."

Jimmy is married to Tina's cousin, Wanda. He's got both chicks mesmerized. His wife calls him the Climax Kid, and Tina refers to him as Metronome Fuck, "He'll keep on ticking as long as you want," Jimmy's wife is quite different from her cousin, Tina. First of all, Wanda respects her husband and their marriage vows—she does not engage in extra-marital sexual activity. Secondly, she does not believe that a blow-job is simply an act of friendship or a meaningless method to become one of the crowd. Lastly, she loves her husband deeply and will be at his side until, "death do them part." Tina on the other hand is everything that most women consider loathsome—a self-centered hussy with no conscience.

It's probably time to tell you a little bit about Tina's mouth fixation. This phenomenon is the instinctual craving or drive behind human activities, especially the energy associated with sexual instinct. We will heretofore refer to this psychic energy as, "The Blow-Job."

Several months ago the police department presented a seminar for its cops relating to racial profiling. The seminar was conducted as part of a court-ordered consent decree. Knowing that Jimmy and most of the Rhoidsville cops would be in attendance, Tina showed up. Initially one would think that her attendance at this session made no sense, however, if one remembers the mouth fixation, everything comes into focus. From the time she arrived and until the seminar was almost over, she talked to all of the guys about having a few drinks after the training, kind of like a graduation party. Little did anyone realize that her libido was in high gear.

The entire group, except for Tina's husband and Jimmy migrated to a local tavern after the seminar. Tommy didn't go, because at work tomorrow the embarrassment would be dreadfully painful—he had been through this before. Jimmy didn't go, because he promised his wife, Wanda, that he would take her to the movies that evening. That night Tina drank shots, fondled dicks, and for a commencement finale, furnished a blow-job smorgasbord for the boys.

The next day when Jimmy arrived at the police station, he noticed the animal van parked at the department kennel. He walked over and saw that Tina was there in her uniform skirt, cleaning some cages. There was only one stray housed at this time, a large Doberman pinscher.

When Jimmy walked in, Tina was bent over ringing out a mop, the uniform skirt she was wearing slid up, exposing her nicely rounded ass, which was bare except for a pair of white panties, provocatively tucked into the crack of her butt. Jimmy said, Hey, doll, hold that pose."

Tina, obeying Jimmy's request, held her pose, looked over her shoulder at him, smiled, and positioned her feet further apart. While in this pose, Tina supported herself by leaning on one of the chain link cages with her left-hand. She slid her right hand into her panties and began fondling herself, while she slowly rotated her ass. He said, "Show me some skin." Jimmy approached her from behind, unzipped his trousers, and displayed his thick, half-hard prick, which he handled like a big piece of limp sausage. Jimmy slowly pulled Tina's panties over her plus ass and down her legs. When her vagina was exposed, he teasingly slid his huge dick between the wet, soft lips of her cunt and started giving her clitoris a dick massage. Tina moaned as she pushed backwards into Jimmy, "Don't tease me, Zizzo, I want you in me now." She was very wet and her clitoris felt like a small marble in oil.

Jimmy was fully erect now, ten inches long, and about four inches in diameter. He put his hand on Tina's shoulders and straightened her upright. They walked over to an equipment table, Jimmy positioned Tina on the table so that her ass was right on the edge, again he began testing, rubbing the large head of his prick against her clit and between the soaked lips of her vagina. Tina grabbed the back of Jimmy's trousers, trying to pull him into her, being mindful of where they were, Jimmy kept his trousers on. Tina's wetness was now running down the cheeks of her ass and onto the table. Jimmy lifted each of her legs over his shoulders, Tina was not a tall girl and, therefore, her legs were pointed straight up. As Jimmy entered her, he was methodical, using long deep strokes and a steady rhythm. After about ten minutes, Jimmy picked up the pace until he was giving Tina a jackknife ram fuck and had her pussy popping like Yucatan chewing gum. She had several orgasms in rapid succession, Jimmy was thicker than ever as his dick plunged in and out of Tina, the shaft glistening from her incredible wetness.

During this half-hour of frenzied fucking, neither of them had noticed the Doberman watching the show. Jimmy could hold back no longer and with deep surges, he exploded into Tina. When he withdrew, Tina's vagina was still contracting, causing Jimmy's cum to stream down the crack of her ass. With her eyes closed, Tina whispered, "Jimmy, a girl could get used to this. You've got me spoiled—I don't get this at home, but I think I'll get out of my situation soon. Why don't you do the same, so we can really get it on?"

Jimmy smiled and said, "I don't think so." He straightened

himself out and headed into work. Tina slid off the table and walked to the cage containing her only guest, the Doberman. She had caught the dog before, but he had never given her any trouble. Tina entered the cage to give him some food and water, but when she bent over to fill the water bowl, her skirt slid up, exposing that plump, wet ass. The big Doberman wasted no time, eagerly mounting her from behind. Tina didn't know what to do—she was breathless and speechless and the dog was big, probably 75 pounds. He knocked Tina down so that she was now on her hands and knees. He then positioned his front paws over her shoulders, his lean skinny hard-on slid up and down her cum-soaked ass until it found the brown-eye. What followed was a whopping butt fuck.

When the salad toss was over, Tina locked the dog in his cage. He was exhausted, just sitting there panting. She picked up a phone and dialed Jimmy's extension. When he answered she said, "Get your ass back over here NOW."

Jimmy didn't get a chance to speak, because Tina slammed the phone down. Upon his return to the kennel, Tina told Jimmy the whole story and ended it with, "I want you to put that mother-fucker down. SHOOT HIM RIGHT NOW!"

Jimmy not knowing what to do, asked, "Do we know who the owner is?"

Tina glared at him and said, "What's the difference? Are you going to do this thing for me or are you a half-dick like my husband?" Jimmy reluctantly upholstered his side arm, a 9 mm Glock, and put three shots into the seated docile canine.

As it turned out, the dog was owned by one Hermann

Goebbles, a dog breeder. The Doberman that Jimmy murdered was a three-time winner in his breed at the American Kennel Society's dog of the year contest. Rhoidsville eventually settled with Mr. Goebbles for approximately $250,000. In case, you're interested, the dog's name was Joseph Paul. Jimmy never fully realized how much his actions had endeared Tina to him—multiple orgasms and heroics were everything she ever wanted in her man.

Chapter 8

"The Song of Love Is A Sad Song ... "

RIGHT AFTER THE FIRST OF THE NEW YEAR, TOMMY REARDON was released by his doctor to return to work. His stroke, although not to be ignored, was minor. As a matter of fact, the paralysis he experienced immediately after the attack is gone. Tommy spent several weeks in the hospital undergoing various tests and therapy. His fellow detectives visited him regularly, but seldom had his wife, and never his father-in-law—he had no other family nearby.

Tommy wished his wife would have come around more often and on one occasion, he told her so over the telephone, "Honey, I wish I could see you more."

Tina's response to her husband's request was, "Well, Tommy, you know what they say—if you put a wish in one hand and spit in the other what have you got? Anyway, when you do get home we need to talk about us."

"What's this all about, Tina?"

"We'll talk when you get home." Tina was setting the stage—she wanted out, as she no longer had any use for a whimpering coward. She was sure that her husband did not have the stomach for a fight, and if she could make his life miserable, he would want out. What she overlooked was that no matter what, he loved her—loved her enough to endure any indignity.

The doctor's orders for Tommy were few and simple. First, take one five milligram pill of Coumadin per day, this medication is an anticoagulant. Lastly, get a blood test once a month to monitor the Coumadin therapy. Tommy took his medicine regularly, but never complied with the ordered blood tests.

On his first day home from the hospital, Tina met him at the front door, "You look OK, rested, so don't expect me to wet nurse you." He just smiled and blew her a kiss. If he only knew how many times she was out sucking and fucking while he was in the hospital, his homecoming might have been a little more spirited.

Day after day for weeks, Tina constantly insulted and degraded Tommy in many ways, but the most devastating of her contemptuous strategies was telling him that she had to gratify herself sexually with others after their marriage, because he simply, "can't cut it." Tommy continued to courageously muddle through, blaming himself for Tina's confessed adultery. He realized that she was flirtations, tempestuous, and sometimes unrestrained, but he would have never imagined her grudge fucking. With his guilt level at a new high, he continuously asked himself, "How could I do this to her?" As for Tina, she was also at wits ends, "What do I need to do to get rid of this asshole?"

While getting ready to go to work one morning, Tina observed Tommy's pill bottle in the medicine cabinet. The brand name of his medicine is Coumadin, but the product is also referred to as warfarin. The bottle had the word

WARNING on it in large gold letters. The warning specified that the medication could be extremely dangerous and never take more than instructed to by your doctor. Also, in bold print on the bottle was the warning, **Limit intake of alcohol**. The instructions on the bottle directed Tommy to take one five milligram pill every morning.

Tina needed to do some research, so she called the police department looking for Jimmy. Instead, she ended up talking to Ted Bielecki, since Jimmy was out with her husband working on a case. Tina asked Ted, "Hey, you guys have a book about drugs, don't you?"

"Yeah we do, it's called da PDR." Teddy was referring to the Physician's Desk Reference, a book commonly used by police to identify pills and capsules.

Tina asked, "Look up Coumadin—a friend of mine wants to know if it's dangerous, you know, like real dangerous."

After a few minutes Teddy responded, "Found it, it's an Anti something or udder, and tell your friend its real dangerous, looks like it could kill ya."

Tina discovered that there were about forty-three pills in the bottle, as this particular prescription had just been filled two days ago. Tommy cooked dinner every night—Tina never did, and she usually went out in the evening. While Tommy cooked, he would have a few glasses of red wine and two or three more glasses at dinner. Tina's plan regarding Tommy suddenly changed, as this new strategy would be a sure, quick way to freedom for her.

The more she thought about it, the more appealing it became. For example, a byproduct to this scenario was her husband's pension—Tina would be entitled to a widow's pension. She started to organize a plan of action. First, how would she facilitate an overdose? She noticed that the pills could be ground up, so she could probably put it in his wine. She also had to make him believe that she wanted to salvage their marriage. Tina planned to stay home every night and be the doting housewife—this would also give her the opportunity to spot symptoms, whatever they may be, but she envisioned stomach cramps, dizziness, and nausea. She rationalized that the pills were Tommy's prescription, so nobody could connect her to them or Tommy's overdose. She also had to rehearse her sorrow at losing the love of her life.

She put the new plan into action immediately by removing two pills from the bottle. They were small and orange in color, so she figured the thing to do is crush them and put the residue into his wine. What could be used to do the grinding? She started looking around the house and found a shot glass. The pills could be crushed in the glass and it is small enough to be kept in her purse every day. Now something was needed to do the actual grinding. As she rummaged through drawers, she found a thimble, which is "perfect," both the glass and thimble could be easily concealed in the purse, too.

Tina did not go to work this day, but called in sick— she had some planning to do. She called Tommy at work, "Honey, I'm staying home today. I have a headache, but will you be home for dinner? I'm broiling a couple of steaks."

Tommy, surprised as hell, responded, "OK, I'll be home around six."

Tina greeted him at the door with a hug and a big kiss, "Oh Tommy, I have been so wrong, can you ever forgive me?"

"Tina I love you, always have." She smiled and simultaneously started fondling his penis, she pushed him into an armchair in the parlor and gave him a great blow-job.

Afterwards Tina rose to her feet from the kneeling position and asked, "How about some vino, honey?"

"Sounds good to me." Tina walked quickly into the kitchen, where she had two ground pills ready to go. She put the residue into a wine glass and dissolved it with burgundy wine.

Earlier during the day Tina found an old brochure that had been circulated by the Rhoidsville Fire Department describing some of the symptoms associated with poisoning. The pamphlet warned about headaches, stomach cramps, diarrhea, vomiting, and choking. She would watch for the symptoms. Tina served Tommy his Coumadin-laced wine, which he drank down quickly. She broiled two steaks, prepared a nice salad, and two baked potatoes. They had dinner, more wine, watched TV, went to bed and made love.

The days that followed were reruns of the first. During this time Tommy showered Tina with flowers, candy, and jewelry. She was hoping to see more symptoms soon. Ten days had passed, but Tommy never once winced, complained of pain, or even burped.

Better increase the dosage, she thought to herself, but she was running low on pills. Tommy was taking his prescribed one-a-day and she was crushing another two into his wine daily. Any time now he would notice that his medication is depleting too quickly, so she had to work fast. Tina recalled that their pharmacy had a computerized express prescription refill service. If she used this program, she did not have to talk to a person—she merely needed to follow the prompts on the computer menu, all of this was accomplished over the phone and she was back in business.

After Tina picked up another forty-five pills at the drugstore, she decided to increase the pill grinding routine to three per day. "This crap has to take hold soon." She could not believe that he was not writhing in pain or puking his guts out. Instead, she was sucking his dick every day and he fucked her every night. She mused to herself, "Maybe I'll have to fuck him to death." She quickly refocused, "Fuck him to death my ass, if he doesn't weaken soon, I'll have to shoot him." Tina's strategy continued for another two weeks, so practically a month had passed with Tommy receiving over triple the prescribed dose of Coumadin.

The fact that Tommy was not reacting to the huge overdoses the way Tina envisioned caused her to begin some introspection. First of all, she has never been showered with as much affection, tenderness, and understanding by anyone. What has she been thinking about for the last five years— this guy adores her and always has, yet she chose to play with his head and now try to kill him. She's beginning to think that her husband's resistance to the poisonous levels of Coumadin may be the result of fate, and if her destiny is to continue in a relation with Tommy, so be it. He had made her feel respectable and wanted. Tina thinks to herself, "I'm in love with this guy. If he's the worst thing that ever happens to me, I'm a lucky girl. Thank God, Tommy warded off that shit I was pumping into him. I nearly destroyed the best thing that ever happened to me."

When Tina took her lunch break at home, she removed everything from her purse, with the exception of the shot glass and thimble. She proceeded to the police department kennel, where she threw the purse into a trashcan. Seeing that purse with its contents in the garage seemed to take tremendous pressure off of her.

Chapter 9

"How Do You Like Me Now Daddy?"

UNFORTUNATELY TINA NEVER LEARNED ENOUGH ABOUT Tommy's medication. Coumadin (warfarin) is a powerful anti-coagulant, a blood thinner. When people are taking Coumadin, it is very important to monitor levels of the drug in their system regularly. This is accomplished with a blood test called a "PT" or "INR". These tests help to determine the amount of warfarin that one needs to take. Although ordered to do so by his doctor, Tommy never fully complied with this testing. While he was in the hospital due to his stroke, it was determined that an effective and safe dose of this medicine for Tommy was not more than five milligrams per day.

On the day that Tina decided to discontinue her insane scheme, she made passionate love to Tommy. The session was so intense that he needed to take a shower. While stepping out of the tub, Tommy took a hard fall, injuring himself on the right side. Although it was painful, his injury appeared minor. In the morning they both noticed that he had considerable bruising on his abdomen, but because there was only moderate pain Tommy and Tina decided not to call the doctor, but instead wait to see how he fared over the next few days.

At work that day Tommy noticed there was some blood in his urine, so he called Tina and she insisted that he call his doctor. Tommy, having had enough of doctors and hospitals and also trying to prove that he was not a wimp, decided to wait, since he was not in unbearable pain or other discomfort. However, he continued to see blood in his urine for over a week.

During this same period, the bruising on his abdomen spread downward into the lower torso. Tina nagged Tommy about seeing his doctor and he decided to do so after several days, because the bruised area had developed a deep purple-green color and now it was much more painful. But that was not the only problem—he felt weak and nauseated every day, accompanied with periods of dizziness. He spared Tina the details regarding the most recent problems, so as not to worry her more. Tina wondered to herself if what she had done was the cause of Tommy's condition, but rationalized that the fall in the tub was responsible.

On one of Tina's days off, a Saturday, she received a phone call from Jimmy Zizzo. He inquired about her husband, because Tommy had taken several days off work. After a short conversation about Tommy and before hanging up, Jimmy said, "Hey, by the way, a couple of weeks ago I was in the kennel and found a purse in the trash can. I looked inside and it had your name written in it. Did you want to throw it out?

"Yes, I did, Jimmy."

"Okay, I'll shit-can it again for you. Take it easy, doll."

After the doctor examined Tommy, he checked him into the hospital immediately. A full examination, which included an MRI, revealed that Tommy's liver was ruptured and hemorrhaging. Because the damaged liver and internal bleeding went untreated for days, infection had set it. The doctors also discovered that his blood was over ten times thinner than should be and that certainly did not help the situation. Tina was informed that even with transfusions, the doctors did not believe they could save Tommy.

When she was finally able to see her husband, he was semi-conscious due to powerful pain killers, but during one waking moment he saw Tina at his side and whispered, "All I ever wanted to do was be your champion." Tina held his hand as he slipped back into a deep sleep.

At this time his doctor entered the room and spoke to Tina, "If Tommy had only gone to the Coumadin Center for testing as I had instructed him to do, and more importantly stuck to his prescribed five milligrams per day, he probably wouldn't be going through this … his blood is well over ten times thinner than it should be."

Tina just looked at the doctor through tear-filled eyes, but she never spoke. The doctor put his hand on her shoulder, "Tina, we'll do everything possible to save him, but we are up against two huge problems: uncontrolled bleeding associated with a major organ and a very, very serious infection." After the doctor walked away, Tina became sick to her stomach when reflecting back on how she intentionally and evil-mindedly overdosed the one person who truly loved her.

When visiting hours were over and upon approaching the ICU exit, Tina observed Jimmy Zizzo and Teddy Bielecki talking to Tommy's doctor at the nurses' station. Exhausted and distressed, she was not in the mood to talk with anyone, so she went home. The next morning, the doctor called Tina at home, "Tina, I feel it's important that you prepare yourself for the worst, as Tommy is not improving. I believe we are losing him and I don't think he'll make it through the day—I'll do my best to keep you informed."

Back at the police department Jimmy Zizzo had a dilemma. Tommy and Jimmy were more than colleagues—they were friends. Tommy's becoming ill almost coincided with Jimmy's discovery of Tina's purse. The day Jimmy found the purse, he had observed her pull up to the kennel, get out of the animal van with her purse, go inside for about half a minute, and return to the van without it. When Jimmy discovered it, he opened the purse. The only contents were the shot glass and thimble, both items along with the inside of the purse were all coated with an orange-colored granular residue.

Tommy's doctor indicated to Jimmy confidentially that he might have misused his medication, causing his blood to thin to a very dangerous level. Jimmy started to organize his thoughts. First, Tommy was not stupid and certainly not laissez faire about his medication. He once mentioned to Jimmy that he had to be careful not to exceed one pill a day, because to do otherwise was very dangerous. Secondly, on numerous occasions, Tina openly told Jimmy and others that she wanted to get out of her marriage.

Jimmy began to analyze his dilemma carefully—on the one hand, he wanted to know what really happened to his friend, while on the other, pursing a hunch might cost him his career. Now comes the issue of the purse—under different circumstances, it would go to the crime lab for analysis. Nobody else except Tina knows about the purse, so if he sends it to the lab and they discover something incriminating then, "Fuck her." If the residue turns out to be nothing, "No harm done."

When he called Tina about the purse, Jimmy never let on that he was suspicious about Tommy's illness. He left her with the impression that he was going to throw it out. Jimmy personally delivered the purse to the crime lab the following day and turned it over to a friend, a forensic chemist, and a nice looking broad that he had dated a few times. He asked her as a favor to process the purse as soon as possible and contact only him with the results. He also mentioned to the chemist the possibility that Coumadin is a factor in the case. Jimmy's friend agreed, but also reminded that what they were doing was a radical departure from the usual course of business, primarily she was referring to a proper paper trail. Jimmy thanked her and said, "I'll wait for your call."

Later that same afternoon, Tina received a call from Tommy's doctor, "He's gone, Tina, we couldn't save, I'm so terribly sorry. If I can help you with anything, don't hesitate to call." Even though she knew he was very ill and in mortal danger, Tina was devastated.

As soon as her father received the news he called, "Well, it never fails—patience pays off, honey. "Don't dis beat divorce proceedings? You are finally rid of da wimp, but I still don't understand what killed him, it sounds like a liver ting. I never tought he was a heavy drinker, go figure." Tina never spoke, she just listened. "Let me know if you need help wit da funeral arrangements, OK?"

"Sure, Dad, I have to go now, so I'll talk to you later."

The next afternoon, Jimmy who was also aware of Tommy's death, received a call from his forensic chemist friend, "I have two things for you, Mr. Ding-Dong. First, there's a readable fingerprint on the shot-glass and second, the orange residue in the purse, the shot glass, and thimble is chemically consistent with Coumadin. Jimmy, please send some paperwork, so I can send you formal lab report."

"OK, princess, and thanks."

Jimmy had to move fast. He called Teddy Bielecki and asked him to come in and witness an interrogation. Teddy asked, "What case is dis, Jim?"

"I'll explain it to you when you come in."

Then Jimmy called Tina at home and instructed her to come into the station.

She responded as though she was expecting his call, "OK, Jimmy, I'll be right in." She recalled the night she observed Jimmy and Teddy talking to her husband's doctor at the hospital, and Jimmy's call about the purse. Normally when she was in trouble she would call her dad or her uncle, Captain Batko, but not this time.

Teddy arrived at the station before Tina, "What's up, Jimbo?"

"Teddy, I can't talk right now, I'm up to my ass in reports. I'll explain as we go along." Jimmy needed to stall his partner, who would no doubt panic if he knew the nature of this investigation and certainly run to the captain.

Tina arrived within minutes, so Jimmy had her sit at his

desk. He asked Teddy to come into the office. Upon seeing Tina, Teddy said, "Sorry about Tommy, kid, I'm at a loss for words."

Jimmy points to a chair and remarks, "Well, when words are lost, it's time to keep quiet. Sit here, Teddy."

Jimmy continues, "Tina, we have to talk about what happened to Tommy. Do you mind if I tape record our conversation?" Jimmy turned on the tape recorder.

At this point, Tina broke down sobbing and put her head on her arms, which were resting on the desk. She then blurted out loudly, "Oh God, what have I done?"

Teddy sat perfectly still, wide-eyed and open mouthed. Jimmy immediately began reading and enumerating to Tina her constitutional rights and warnings, "Tina, you have the right to remain silent … " as Jimmy continued, his recital became obscure to her and his voice faint, the words he spoke quietly resonated in the background of her thoughts and became undiscernible

Tina thought to herself, "I wish I could go back in time, just two months. I wish Tommy was here by my side." Then she remembered when Tommy needed her while he was in the hospital, he phoned, because she never visited, "Tina I wish I could see you more often." She recalled what she told him, "Tommy, if you put a wish in one hand and spit in the other, what have you got?"

Jimmy's voice suddenly became clear again, "Tina Reardon, do you acknowledge, understand, and knowingly waive your rights to remain silent?"

"Yes."

"Will you of your own free will give us a statement of the facts as best as you know them surrounding the death of Thomas Reardon?"

"Yes … yes, I will."

The justice in this case will be legal, that is,
Trial, Finding, Sentencing.
For this defendant, it may prove to be merciless.

CPSIA information can be obtained
at www.ICGtesting.com
Printed in the USA
LVHW010926170520
655736LV00006B/432